DISUNIONIA

A POLITICAL THRILLER

MICHAEL L. WALDEN

DISUNIONIA
A POLITICAL THRILLER

iUniverse books may be ordered through booksellers or by contacting:

iUniverse
1663 Liberty Drive
Bloomington, IN 47403
www.iuniverse.com
844-349-9409

ISBN: 978-1-6632-0224-6 (sc)
ISBN: 978-1-6632-0225-3 (e)

Library of Congress Control Number: 2020913345

Print information available on the last page.

iUniverse rev. date: 08/13/2020

To my late mother, who taught me to work hard, not complain, and to correct my numerous faults.

CHAPTER 1

The Capitol, Washington, DC, Monday, January 3, Early Afternoon

It wasn't what the new Senator from South Carolina expected. Mark Williams had always loved history. As a boy he began reading history books for fun, and the passion continued into adulthood. He even brought along a new biography of John Calhoun on his honeymoon. Perhaps it was because South Carolinians are very sensitive to history. They were the first to fire shots during the Civil War and one of the last to remove the image of the Confederate insignia from the state flag. Mark wanted South Carolina to be remembered better in the future.

The history books Mark had read, and the pictures and videos he had seen, depicted the U.S. Capitol as a magical and majestic building, reminding him of the grand halls and castles of Europe. He had eagerly anticipated stepping into the National Statuary Hall near the Capitol's rotunda, climbing the elegant staircases of burnished oak leading to the building's upper floors, and then walking through the wide hallways as the eyes of historical figures memorialized in portraits on both walls watched him. Even though the January weather was unseasonably warm during his swearing-in that morning, Mark still felt a chill of giddiness knowing he was now a part of the grandeur of the Capitol and the power of the federal government.

When he entered the Hall of Statutes Mark was immediately confronted with a scene that shocked, disappointed and even sickened him. Huey Long's raised right hand was now hanging limply at the statue's side, probably only weeks away from joining the dust and discarded wrappers on the Hall's floor. George Washington's walking stick was shattered, and since it supported the figure's right side, it was only a matter of time before the father of the country toppled over. Yet most troublesome to Mark was his favorite, the statue of Frederick Douglass. Douglass was grasping a lectern with one hand and crushing papers – representing slavery – with the other. The fingers of Douglass' hands were chipped, and the sheath of papers was slowly disintegrating to nothing. Mark wondered if the condition of Douglass' statue was a sign of the future.

Mark took the stairs to the gallery on the second floor overlooking the Senate chamber. He actually had no choice as the elevators were not working. The carpet on the stairway was worn to almost nothing, and the once beautiful banisters had more nicks and chips than polish. On his walk down the hallway Mark noticed numerous portraits either missing or hanging in a lopsided fashion. Perhaps those from the past were trying to return there.

Mark opened one of the gallery doors to take a peek at the floor of the world's most exclusive club – the U.S. Senate. He couldn't wait to see the centuries' old desks once occupied by legends like Daniel Webster, Harry Truman, John Kennedy, and Bob Dole. But with half the chamber's lights not working, both the desks and the few Senators on the floor were just shadowy images.

Trying to prevent disappointment from turning to depression, Mark walked to the basement of the Capitol and took the special subway to his office in the Dirksen office building next to the Capitol. Surely the space where he would conduct much of the important business of his position would be better equipped and certainly clean. He was, after all, a U.S. Senator, one of only one hundred, many of whom thought she or he should be President. The working hub of a Senator had to be comfortable and functional.

But it wasn't, not even close. The name stenciled to his office door should have been a clue. It was actually half a name, and that of the former occupant. Remnants of the other half had been scraped away and dropped to the floor. Once inside Mark noticed peeling paint on the walls, numerous non-functioning lights, and computers that were several generations old. Plus, no one was around. Senators' offices used to be places of constant motion, with staff, lobbyists, colleagues, and constituents always moving in and out. Decades ago, one Senator compared his office to a beehive, with the on-going buzzing of individual bees all trying to get to the queen.

Mark knew Washington had changed. With the two-party system dead and replaced by numerous smaller fragments, it was virtually impossible to form a ruling majority. In addition to the Democrat and Republican parties, ten others – the Tea, Socialist, Libertarian, Globalist, Green, Alt-Right, States Rights, Farmer, LGBTQ, and, somewhat ironically, the Anarchist, – had elected at least one member to Congress. The dominance of Democrats and Republicans was long past, with both parties combined having only 23 members in Congress. With no party anywhere close to a majority, coalitions were constantly forming and fracturing. No continuity of power meant little success in governing. A full federal budget hadn't been passed in over a decade, no Supreme Court Justice had been confirmed in twelve years, and all members of the President's cabinet had the designation "Acting." The federal government was running on fumes.

"Senator Williams, it's so good to see you," shouted a voice that echoed in the tomblike office. Initially startled, Mark turned to see a trim but well-rounded, 40-something year old woman with grey-brown hair approaching him with an outstretched hand. She was professionally dressed in a dark skirt, white blouse, and light brown jacket.

Before Mark could respond the high-energy woman was pumping his hand and giving him a gleaming smile. "I apologize if I surprised you. I'd hoped you'd show up today." She now had a two-handed grasp of Mark's right hand. "I'm Denise Perdue, your administrative secretary. At least, I was the administrative secretary when I started eight years ago. Now I'm the only secretary. So I guess you can leave off the 'administrative' and just say 'secretary.'" Denise let out a giggle as she finished the last rapid-fire sentence.

Denise was impressed with Mark's looks. In contrast to many of the aging, droopy, and wheezing members of the Senate, Mark was trim, with angular features, black hair highlighted with hints of grey, and wore his suit like a professional male model. Denise would look forward to coming to work each morning.

Mark initially wasn't impressed with Denise. She seemed annoyingly friendly and spoke much too fast. Hopefully they'd get along. Indeed, they'd have to get along as there appeared to be no other options. However, one thing about Denise did appeal to him.

"You're from the South, right?" asked Mark.

"Indeed, I am, sir. Born and bred in South Carolina," answered Denise as she lifted her eyes and fluttered her eyelids. She was trying to affect a Scarlet O'Hara accent and attitude.

Mark ignored the theatrics and moved on. "Do I detect an Upstate accent?"

Denise looked confused. "Upstate?"

"Yes, Upstate. You know, in South Carolina we have two distinct dialects, the Low Country along the coast and particularly around Charleston, and the Upstate in the foothills near Greenville and Spartanburg."

"OK, I get it, Upstate. Yes, that's where I'm from."

Smiling, Mark asked, "What town?"

Not hesitating, Denise quickly answered, "Oh, the state capital, Columbia."

"Well, that's not really Upstate. People around there speak more of a blend of Upstate and Low Country that some call Midlands or Midstate. But I guess I'm being picky. Maybe it's because I grew up in Charleston when people there were snobby about residents in the rest of the state. Fortunately that's changed with the growth of USC in Columbia and BMW in Spartanburg-Greenville. Charlestonians have a little bit of envy now for the success of both the Midlands and Upstate."

There was a slight pause as if Denise was deciding what next to say. "Yep, USC, the University of South Carolina, sure is a big place."

Odd answer, thought Mark, but it was time to talk business. "I'll be honest, Denise. I know there's been hard times for the federal government, but I would never have imagined this hard. Now please, don't think I'm blaming you, but this place is filthy. And do the computers even work?"

Now back to her chirpy self, Denise agreed. "Oh, no offense taken, Senator. Can I call you Senator? I don't want to assume anything. This office sure could stand a good cleaning and vacuuming. The problem is there's few people to do it. I think the janitorial staff for the Capitol has been cut by more than half since I've been here. But I'll try to find someone. If not, I'll scurry around for a vacuum and run it myself. And, yes, the computers are old, but they do work. Fortunately, we still have email. If you'll excuse me Senator, off I go to find some help."

Mark was amazed how Denise could merge several thoughts into one long monologue. In a flash she was out the door. Mark plopped down into - what used to be - an expensive executive leather chair with a high back and several comfort settings. Now, rips were everywhere, the cushioning was shot, and the swivel was stuck in one position.

With Denise on her search for cleaners or cleaning implements, Mark could reflect on what brought him to Washington. Mark's father had been a textile executive who encouraged his son to pursue an alternative occupation when the textile industry began moving to Mexico and Asia. His father also preached the learn-earn-serve philosophy of learning an occupation, being financially successful, and then serving in public office. Following his own advice, the elder Williams had won a couple of terms in the South Carolina House of Representatives.

An accountant by training, Mark Williams grew a one-person operation into a statewide powerhouse with offices in all of South Carolina's major cities. He was first elected to the South Carolina House, and then a few years later to the more prestigious South

Carolina Senate. When one of the state's U.S. Senate seats became open, Mark won the primary for the Libertarian Party nomination and faced four other opponents from the Tea, Green, Socialist, and State Rights parties in the general election. With so many parties competing in elections, it was rare the winner achieved a majority of the vote. Such was the case with Mark, where he was triumphant with only 28% of voters casting their ballot for him.

A smile then came across Mark's face. He'd conquered tough challenges before, and he'd do the same as a U.S. Senator. He also had the love of his life – Cheryl – supporting him from their home in Charleston. With two sons now in high school and soon bound for college, Mark and Cheryl had decided their children needed a normal life in surroundings they knew. Mark would visit Charleston on most weekends and during Senate breaks. This was asking a lot of Cheryl, but she was an amazing woman.

Despite the uncomfortable chair, thinking sweet thoughts of his family caused Mark to begin to doze off. He was roused from his bliss by the sound of breaking glass and a loud crashing sound. Mark instinctively dived to the floor under his desk.

CHAPTER 2

The Capitol, Washington, DC, Monday, January 3, Mid Afternoon

MARK DIDN'T MOVE FOR SEVERAL MINUTES. AFTER HEARING NO other sounds, he slowly peered around the corner of the desk, then gently crept out of his hiding place until he was near the office door. Finally rising, he noticed the outside window was cracked, but there was no hole, suggesting the damage was not caused by a bullet.

Mark froze when he heard rapidly paced steps coming closer from the hallway. Then, just as he was about to scramble back to shelter under his desk, there came a now familiar sound, "Senator William, Senator Williams, are you OK? What was that big crash? I don't know what I'd do if something happened to you. The noise reminds me of ….."

It was Denise rambling on even though Mark's life could have been hanging by a thread. Mark emerged from under the desk and Denise ran toward him. Just as it appeared Denise was about to grasp Mark in a bear hug, she stopped short. "Oh, I see what happened," she explained while looking up at the ceiling. "The chandelier finally fell. I knew it was on its last legs. And see here," as Denise pointed to the window, "one of its glass thing-a-ma-gigs flew over to the window and cracked it. I don't know why that chandelier was up there in the first place."

Mark was relieved. His brain had immediately thought the worst by assuming someone had attempted to scare or even harm him. He now felt stupid, ashamed, and cowardly.

Denise was apparently good at reading faces and connecting them to thoughts. "Don't be upset. I would have also thought something bad was happening. But on the upside, I found a vacuum. It's in the outside office. I'll also scrounge around for some cardboard and tape so we can cover that hole in the window. Lord only knows how long it will take to be replaced. And let me go find a large trash can, or better yet, a trash bin, so we can get rid of that fancy light fixture. I'm afraid we're going to have to do almost everything ourselves."

Mark had already begun to collect the pieces of the chandelier as Denise started back to the hallway when they heard, "Hello, hello, anyone home? Senator Williams, are you here?"

Framed by Mark's office door was a stunning 60ish-age Black woman, immaculately dressed in a red pantsuit highlighted by a red, white, and blue scarf and wearing earrings in the shape of the U.S flag. One high heel was red while the other was blue, and a sparkling thick white belt emphasized a pleasing hourglass figure.

"My, my, what's happened here? I hope no one was hurt. I'll have some of my staff come over here to help with the cleanup," the stranger added as she pulled a cell phone from her trouser pocket.

"I'm sorry, but you are…" Mark began.

Denise cut Mark off. "Oh silly, this is the esteemed senior senator from North Carolina, Senator Beatrice Cooley."

Beatrice approached Mark and took his hand. "Please call me Bee. Everyone does. I wanted to come by as soon as I could and officially welcome you to the U.S. Senate. I expect you and I can work together for the good of both Carolinas. After all, we do share the Carolina Panthers. We in North Carolina love it when you South Carolinians come to Charlotte for games and spend all that money." Bee's face broke into a wide grin with the last statement. "And by the way, please excuse my rather gaudy attire. I always dress up for inauguration day. Aren't these earrings just the cat's meow? They were given to me by my grandchildren."

Mark was already liking Bee Cooley. By reputation, Senator

Beatrice Cooley was no stranger to him. She was the first Black woman elected to the U.S. Senate from the South and only the third elected in the nation. Even more, she had always been elected as a Republican. Bee combined a fiscal conservatism appealing to right-of-center voters with a genuine passion for promoting education and economic opportunity ringing true for those left-of-center. The combination was unbeatable. In her last election she took 63% of the vote. But with the Republican Party now virtually non-existent, there was constant speculation what party would back Bee for her next election in two years.

"Bee, I apologize for the mess. Please sit." Mark pulled a chair over to his desk and quickly brushed the seat with his handkerchief to remove the deepening dust and any stray shards from the chandelier.

Bee accepted the seat. "There's certainly no need to apologize. My office would look the same if I didn't pay for some extra staff out of my own pocket. I employ several local individuals and have given them opportunities they might never have had. I'm sure they have friends who would work for you if you could arrange the funding."

"Thanks, and I'll certainly consider that. Would you like something to drink? I think we can arrange coffee."

"Thank you. Yes, I would like some coffee. And I might even fortify it with a little something I have in my pocket." Bee tapped a pocket on the right side of her jacket.

Denise had been lingering and listening to the conversation. "Denise, I think I saw a coffee maker in your outside office. Can you make coffee for Senator Cooley and me? And as you go, please close the door."

"Right away Senator. I'll get right on that coffee and have it to you in a jiffy. We'll clean up and cover the window later. So nice to see you Senator Cooley." Denise gave a small wave as she left.

"She appears to be competent but a little too eager, at least by my standards," Mark offered to Bee.

Bee held up her right index finger to signal a point. "But I'll take eagerness over laziness any day. In my experience, you can moderate eagerness more easily than you can reduce laziness."

"I agree." Mark felt a slight bit of inferiority in the presence of someone so obviously accomplished and wise.

"Mark – I hope I can call you Mark – I'm glad we're alone now, because there's a reason other than extending a welcome that brought me to your office. It is to discuss what I consider to be the most dangerous threat confronting our nation today. That threat is Concon."

"Concon?" Mark was bewildered.

Bee edged her chair closer to Mark and leaned in with a sense of urgency. "Concon is short for constitutional convention. There are powerful forces in the country that want to call a constitutional convention so they can dismantle the country. They want to effectively end the United States of America." Bee emphasized her statement with a fist thrust timed to each syllable.

Mark was impressed with the strength and seriousness with which Bee spoke her words. As she talked her eyes narrowed and were unflinching. Mark wouldn't want to debate Bee Cooley. She was confident and captivating; a real leader. Mark was silent and just observed.

"How can they do this, you might ask?" continued Bee. Amazing, thought Mark. She even knows the question I was afraid to ask. Bee immediately answered her own question. "They have two coordinated efforts. One is to get the required number of states to call for a constitutional convention. They already have 30 of the necessary 38. Most of the holdouts are in the South and West."

Denise knocked and brought in the coffee. Bee stopped talking. Mark thanked Denise, but she stayed, as if awaiting orders. "That will be all for now, Denise. Again, please close the door on your way out." Denise uttered 'yes sir,' gave – what looked like – a curtsy with a nod to Bee and Mark, and left.

"Care for a hit? I like a little vodka with my coffee, especially when I'm discussing serious matters." Bee had removed a flask from her jacket pocket and poured a couple of drops into the coffee cup. Mark declined the offer.

Unphased, Bee continued. "The second effort is here in

Washington. Although there is disagreement among legal scholars, the Constitution appears to give Congress the authority to set the rules states must follow to authorize a convention. Up to now the assumed rule has been a state must have a majority of the members in each chamber of their legislature to vote for the conventional convention. Now that the movement to get more states to call for the convention has stalled, there are forces in Congress who want to lower the threshold to 40% voting for the convention. If that happens, I think there'll be enough states to authorize the convention."

Mark felt embarrassed he hadn't heard about Concon. "I guess I heard a few rumblings about this during the campaign, but it never came up as an issue, at least not in debates or in ads."

Bee took a deep, satisfying, sip of her coffee. "That's because the Concon movement is weakest in the South. It's ironic most of the states of the old confederacy want to keep the union. There are some cynics who say that's because poor Southern states benefit most from social programs like Medicare, Food Stamps, and Social Security which are heavily funded by richer states in the North and West. But they're wrong. They're using obsolete, outdated data. In the last twenty years there's been a big shift of economic power and wealth out of the North – especially from states like New York and Massachusetts – and out of Western states like California, to the South. Charlotte is now the financial capital of the country, and a big chunk of the film industry has migrated to Atlanta. It's all about costs. New York, Massachusetts, and California, with their high taxes and massive regulations, have just priced themselves out of the market. Plus, to make matters worse for them, the 2020 Pandemic motivated many to leave the big, dense mega-cities of the Northeast and California where the virus easily spread."

"So how would a constitutional convention help states like New York and California?"

There was another sip of the vodka-coffee mix. "I knew you'd asked that, and it's a great question." Bee certainly is a good politician, thought Mark. Always compliment the questioner. "With the current deal, that is, the Constitution, the federal government controls interstate commerce. Therefore, a state losing workers and businesses can't stop them, unless they change their policies, which most haven't. There's actually rumors some states are thumbing their noses at the depleted federal government and restricting movement of people and firms leaving their states, but I don't know if that's true. Anyway, the Concon backers want a different deal giving states more control and the federal government less control. I think – but not everyone agrees with me – that they want to tear up the Constitution and let each state effectively become an individual country."

Mark was now feeling more confident. Maybe Bee had telepathically loaned him some of her strength. "Wouldn't 50 states be unmanageable? Sure, a state like California could function as a country. It's big enough. But what about Nevada, Kansas, or even South Carolina?"

Mark noticed some hesitancy before Bee had another round of vodka-coffee. Maybe the vodka was affecting her. Still, she went on. "The thought is we wouldn't have fifty countries. Many of the states would form associations or even merge. Some might be motivated to affiliate in some way with foreign countries. That last possibility really scares me. The important point is, there are forces that want to break up the United States as you and I know it. And I hope you will ….will …. join …. me … in ….." Bee abruptly dropped her coffee cup.

Mark jumped up to steady her. "Bee, Bee, are you feeling ill?" Bee was conscious and her eyes open. But Mark felt her body going limp as she began to slide down the chair to the floor.

"Denise, Denise," Mark yelled. Denise came rushing in. "Call 911 or EMS, or whomever you call here for medical emergencies."

"Well, let me think …"

"Damn it Denise, just get some medical help. I don't care from where. I think Senator Cooley has had a heart attack or stroke."

Slowly but firmly Bee raised her right arm to around Mark's neck and pulled him close to her face. With barely a whisper she said, "Files, get the files."

Bees eyes went blank, her mouth opened, and her body froze. Mark quickly felt for a pulse. There was none. Bee Cooley was dead.

CHAPTER 3

The State Capitol, Phoenix Arizona, Monday, January 3, Mid Afternoon

"I do solemnly swear that I will support the Constitution of the United States and the Constitution and laws of the State of Arizona, and that I will bear faith and allegiance to the same and defend them against all enemies, foreign and domestic, and that I will faithfully and impartially discharge the duties of the office of Governor according to the best of my ability, so help me God."

With that statement, Theresa Vargas become the 32nd Governor of the State of Arizona. As she hugged her mother, daughter, and siblings, applause broke out along with some scattered boos. Theresa was actually pleased. As the first non-U.S. citizen to be the Governor of Arizona, Theresa was worried protests would force the inauguration to be held in a smaller venue where the crowd could be controlled.

She also realized the jeers likely came from two factions. One was those who didn't want her to be Governor due to her citizenship status. They resented all Arizona politicians who amended the state constitution several years ago to allow non-U.S. citizens to hold state and local offices. The second group booed because Theresa promised to uphold the U.S. Constitution. This faction was part of the growing movement to call a new national constitutional convention with the ultimate goal of scrapping the Constitution.

When Theresa looked at her beaming mother, Maria, she thought about how far her family had come and how difficult the struggle had been. Maria's husband and Theresa's father Eugenio illegally entered the U.S. forty years ago when Theresa was only five. Theresa was therefore a 'DACA' (Deferred Action for Children Arrivals) child. She has permission to stay in the U.S., but her federal status is still temporary. In the last thirty years there had been many failed attempts to give DACA children a path to citizenship on the basis their illegal entry into the U.S. was not of their own free will. Theresa's two brothers, Luis and Armando, were born in the U.S. and therefore were automatic citizens. So was her daughter Flores.

Eugenio came from a family of carpenters in Mexico. Eugenio put those skills to good use in his new country, beginning as a framer, then working his way up to manager of a framing party, and then finally to general manager of Arizona's largest construction firm. Unfortunately, a family history of coronary disease ended Eugenio's life at the relatively young age of 63.

Pushed by her mother, Theresa excelled in school. Although she did well in all subjects, Theresa was particularly drawn to math and science and especially to physics. Perhaps it was her father's 'construction gene' – as Theresa called it – that ultimately led her to a degree in civil engineering from the University of Arizona. Theresa joined a firm in Phoenix and quickly moved up the company ladder.

But broader, public issues were always on Theresa's mind. Economically comfortable with a young daughter from a passionate, yet eventually unsuccessful, relationship in college, Theresa reduced her time with the engineering firm and ran for a state Senate seat after the amendment to the state Constitution allowing non-U.S. citizen to be officeholders. She was elected three times with overwhelming majorities. Theresa developed a reputation for addressing business concerns about tax rates and striving for efficiency and results in public programs, but in both cases with a focus on providing support and opportunity for those at the bottom of the economic ladder to move up.

It was just a matter of time before Theresa was recruited to run for Governor. The campaign was tough, and – as in most states – she faced multiple opponents. But she had the correct message, and her coalition and voter-turnout operation were strong. Theresa triumphed with 55% of the vote, something unheard of in today's fractured party system.

Theresa attended several inaugural parties, giving handshakes, hugs, and back slaps to countless people. Many of them she didn't personally like, but they could be necessary allies for her agenda. Particularly unpleasant was the fake friendliness she displayed to Senator Tom Ellington, leader of the movement to have Arizona approve the call for a constitutional convention.

"Governor, congratulations." Ellington gave Theresa a tight hug which she couldn't wait to be finished. "I want to get on your calendar as soon as we can to discuss the importance to Arizona of calling for a national constitutional convention. Arizona is being held back by this antiquated document. I know you're not there yet, but with a little reasoning and counseling, we can work together to make the necessary changes to allow Arizona to reach its full potential."

What 'BS' thought Theresa. The Concon movement had a significant following in Arizona, so she had to bite her tongue during the campaign and tiptop around the issue. She wasn't proud of this tactic, but she accepted the need, knowing once in office she'd do everything she could to hold off Concon.

However, Theresa couldn't afford to make Ellington an enemy right now, so she displayed a false smile. "Tom, I look forward to discussing this key issue with you and others. I know we all want what's best for Arizona. I want to see where the people of Arizona stand. I also want to discuss the question with other governors, particularly those in the West. I've always thought that discussion, reasoning, and evaluation are the best steps to solving any problem."

Ellington knew he was getting the brush-off, and he knew that – although she hid it – Theresa was opposed to Concon. But it was early, and there were many ways to convince even a Governor of the correct position. Now wasn't the time or place to confront Theresa.

"I agree, and I anxiously await reasoning with you on the logic and necessity of the convention. I'll have our staffs talk."

Note to self, thought Theresa. Warn staff to be ready for Ellington's people. Fortunately, there was a line of people waiting to congratulate Theresa, so Ellington moved on.

Three hours after she officially became Governor, Theresa was escorted to her office. With the exception of Alaska and Hawaii, Arizona was the youngest state in the Union, having been admitted in 1912. Its capitol building therefore didn't have the history and legacy of those in many other states. The Governor's office was comfortable, but not really special. Dark wood paneling dominated the room, and the Governor's desk was made of matching wood with a gold trim around the edges. There was a large window behind the desk which allowed ample sunlight and 100-degree heat to permeate the chambers during the state's long summers. Maybe the plan was for the dark wood to absorb the heat rays. Unfortunately, the view from the window was of nondescript buildings and a downtown highway.

After her executive secretary Emily showed Theresa the ropes of the phone, computer, and secure line to the State Police, Theresa dismissed her and settled in for a little quiet time and reflection. Then it finally hit her that she was the Governor, so she allowed herself a fist pump and a muffled 'alright.'

There were several pieces of mail on the desk. Theresa leafed through them but just didn't have the energy or inclination to read them now. Except for one piece. The envelope was standard letter size, but what stood out was its beige color. The lettering of the address was in old English script, and there was no return address.

For the first time, Theresa took her formal Arizona Governor's letter opener and slit the back of the beige envelope. She immediately noticed the paper of the enclosed letter was also beige. Fancy she thought. Unfolding the letter revealed four simple lines:

'Concon is Arizona's only hope. Support Concon. We're watching. You can be a leader, or you can be sorry.'

CHAPTER 4

The Capitol, Washington, DC, Monday, January 3, Late Afternoon

It took an hour for the Capitol Police and EMS to arrive at Mark's office. It was a good thing Bee had died instantly, thought Mark. Otherwise there would have been a hell of a lawsuit.

Denise had used the time to tidy up the office. She never wanted to make a bad impression on anyone, even the Capitol Police, for anything she controlled, and she considered Senator Williams' office her domain. She especially wanted to rid the office of the damaged and broken chandelier. All the debris she put in a large black garbage bag and carted it to the incinerator in the basement of the Capitol Building.

Lt. Evers of the Capitol Police headed the team of investigators and medical personnel. Evers was ex-military, retiring after twenty years of service and then returning to work in the related field of law enforcement. It was a common path for military professionals. Still fit and ramrod straight, Evers displayed a no-nonsense attitude. People reflexively didn't want to cross him.

Bee's body was carefully placed in a body bag and removed. Mark had put his suit jacket over her torso, being careful not to disturb anything. Evers assured Mark he hadn't. Importantly, the flask of vodka was still inside Bee's coat pocket.

"Now, Senator Williams, where is the cup used for the coffee Senator Cooley drank?"

Mark looked at Denise and immediately knew there was a problem. "Gosh, Lt. Evers, those were Styrofoam cups," exclaimed Denise. "Senator Cooley and Senator Williams both used one. I never thought to keep them."

Evers was annoyed. "So what did you do with them?" he firmly asked.

"I took them and all the other trash in the office, including the chandelier that fell – see the hole in the ceiling – to the incinerator in the Capitol Building basement."

"Jenkins, rush down to the incinerator and retrieve that bag," Evers commanded.

"Yes sir," Jenkins replied. "Right away."

Looking down at the floor so she didn't have to look at either Mark or Evers, Denise clarified, "Eh, Lt. Evers, that won't help because the incinerator was running. I think it may run all day. That bag of trash is probably all dust by now."

"Jenkins, stop." Evers face was a mass of anger. His eyes looked as if he was shooting darts. "Ms. ----"

"Perdue," Denise quickly answered. "But everyone calls me Denise."

"Ms. Perdue, do you realize what you've done? You may have destroyed evidence that will help us determine why Senator Cooley died, and, more importantly, if she was murdered."

Denise's eyes were still affixed to the floor. They were also beginning to fill with tears.

"I didn't mean to destroy evidence. I really didn't. You've got to believe me. I am a proud, law-abiding citizen of South Carolina and the United States of America. I have never even received a speeding ticket."

Mark approached Evers. "Lt. Evers, I know Denise made a terrible mistake, but I can assure you it was unintentional. Denise often acts before she thinks. I can't imagine anything coming from this office that would have harmed Senator Cooley. My focus would be on the vodka flask, and fortunately you have that."

Evers had cooled down. "You're probably right, Senator. We'll get the flask to the lab right away. In the meantime, don't discard anything from this office. And if you have any ideas who might have wanted to harm Senator Cooley, please contact me immediately. Here's my card."

"Thanks, and I will, Lt. Evers. I just met Senator Cooley. In fact, I was just sworn in today. So I may not be much help on any enemies she might have. But if I turn up anything, I'll certainly pass it on to you."

Evers nodded, gathered his team, and left. On his way out, he made sure to glare at Denise.

Denise came running to Mark. "Oh, Senator Williams, I am so, so, so sorry. With all the mess and turmoil in the office, my brain just wasn't working at top speed. Do you think I'll be in trouble? I don't think that Lieutenant liked me very much." Denise was working hard to hold back tears.

"I think you'll be fine, Denise. But in the future, tell me what you're going to do before you do it, even if it's something as trivial as taking out the trash."

"You can be sure of that," sniffed Denise. "I'm going to turn over a new leaf and think before I act."

"That's the attitude. Now I have something to tell you that I didn't share with Lt. Evers. It's something Senator Cooley wanted me to do, and I think I owe it to her to do it."

"What's that?" The tears were gone and Denise's face was lit up in anticipation of Mark's answer.

"Just before she died, Senator Cooley whispered to me the words, "files, get the files."

"Files," repeated Denise.

"Yes, files. I'm guessing she knew she would be dead soon, and maybe there are clues in her files as to who may have murdered her."

"You think she was murdered?" Mark couldn't tell if Denise was appalled or excited over the prospect.

"That's my guess now. Of course, I'm an accountant and not a doctor or policeman. But Senator Cooley acted and looked very fit and cogent. I'm betting poison will be found in her flask."

"Poison, wow? A real live murder took place in this office just feet from me. I declare, I never thought I'd live to see that."

Mark inwardly smiled. The real Denise was back. Still, there was a problem. "If there are clues in Senator Cooley's files, then I have two questions. First, what kind of files, paper or digital? And second, how do we get to the files?"

"Senator, I think I can help with both questions." The real Denise really was back.

CHAPTER 5

New York State near the Pennsylvania border, Monday, January 3, Late Afternoon

"You're sure Jason will be there when we arrive?"

Somewhat annoyed that Carol had already asked this question four times in the last two hours, Tony bit his tongue and responded in a calm tone.

"Yes, he will. Jason is very reliable. Remember we shared time in Afghanistan in '22 before we convinced the Indians to move in. The Indians thought they could use that God-forsaken country to surround the Pakis. By now, I bet they wished they never set foot there." Tony thought a short stroll down memory lane would distract his history-expert wife Carol from the danger that was ahead.

For a short time it seemed to work. Carol's Ph.D. was in British history. "I read the other day the Indians are trying to get the British to help them in Afghanistan. It's like the boys from the old British Empire are getting back together." Carol punctuated her remarks with a little chuckle. Tony was pleased.

Their twelve-year old Subaru Forrester continued southwest on Interstate 88 toward Binghamton. The plan was to skirt the New York-Pennsylvania border to Corning, then cross the border on US Rt. 15. Although the crossing was guarded, it was less so than other interstate crossings, especially I-95. Taking I-87 and then linking to I-95 would have been their most direct path from Schenectady, but they couldn't risk the heavily travelled highways. Plus, Jason was part of the New York Border Patrol at Rt. 15. He promised to fix the right-most gate so it would automatically swing up as they approached at the agreed-upon time of 6 pm. He also said at that time most of the guards would be taking an after-dinner nap.

Once in Pennsylvania, the next step was to pick up Interstate 81 at Harrisburg and follow it through Maryland, West Virginia, and finally Virginia. Then they would switch to I-77 and finally I-40 on the way to their ultimate destination of Raleigh, North Carolina. They had friends there who claimed the large number of colleges and universities as well as tech firms should give ample job opportunities for the historian Carol and the tech expert Tony.

Pennsylvania had only recently joined the Northeast Association of States. The main goal of the Association was preventing the out-migration of workers and businesses, with border control being a big part of the restrictions. People leaving the Association's states could not do so without documented permission. But since Pennsylvania had just become a member, the state had few border posts up and running, so I-81 was expected to be unguarded. Maryland, West Virginia and Virginia were not part of the Northeast Association, hence there were no barriers at their borders.

Carol was back to revisiting her worries. "Tony, I'm still concerned this won't work. With our pay constantly being cut at home, I know we were getting poorer. So don't get me wrong. I wanted to leave New York, even though we both were born and raised there and most of our families still live there. But at least we weren't starving, and your dad always brought wood over in the winter so we wouldn't freeze. What if we get caught and are put in jail? With the massive cutbacks, I've read horrible stories of the conditions in New York state prisons. At least if we had stayed home, we'd be free – well, sort of."

Tony grabbed for his coffee mug. Given the time they'd been on the road and with the winter sky now pitch black, Tony felt his eyelids getting a little heavy. Hopefully the caffeine would thwart the desire to sleep.

Fortunately, Tony revived with the jolt of coffee. "Carol, you know we've been over this a hundred times. Things were only getting worse in New York. Nothing works. The schools are losing teachers. Potholes from the winter snows aren't fixed. We only get mail once a week. This is why companies and workers were fleeing south, to Virginia, the Carolinas, and Georgia, or even going overseas, until the state stepped in to seal the borders. Look at you. You have a Ph.D. in history and the best job you could find was loading pastry trucks at 4 am. And then there's me. I have a master's degree in logistics, training which the experts say is the best there is for the future. And what was I doing? Hammering tails for a construction firm that couldn't even afford nail guns."

"You're right, honey, you're right." Carol sounded drowsy. They'd already been up almost 14 straight hours, packing and saying goodbyes to family and friends before they hit the road. And they had many hours yet to go.

"Carol, I need you awake. You can sleep later. I just turned south on 15. We're only a half hour from the border. If we get through, we're home free."

Carol took a couple gulps of coffee and now felt wide awake. Neither talked. They thought about how their lives had changed, almost all of a sudden, so it seemed. It started with New York using the advancements made in AI – artificial intelligence – to create what it claimed was a perfectly planned economy. No more would consumers or companies have to cope with changing prices linked to unexpected fluctuations in supply and demand. AI could turn the unexpected into the expected, predict the price changes before they happened, and then rapidly move resources to prevent the fluctuations from occurring in the first place. The inaccurate and imprecise actions and reactions of firms, investors, and buyers would be replaced by the sure and steady hand of New York's AI Central Economic Planning Model, or AI-CEPM for short!

But AI-CEPM didn't work for two big reasons that the central planners wouldn't admit. First, even the best of the AI models was only 70% accurate, meaning there was always a 30% error rate, which when compounded over time could become gigantic. Second, New

York had imposed many mandates on businesses for coverage of parental leave, shorter workdays, longer vacations, and pollution controls. The central planners expected the costs of these mandates to be taken from company profits, and authorities wouldn't allow them to be reflected in product prices or workers' wages. However, the mandates and price controls put New York companies at a competitive disadvantage compared to companies in other states, which, in turn motivated the companies to shut down or leave.

The outmigration of companies and workers is what caused New York and several other states – mostly in the Northeast – that adopted AI-CEPM to impose the border controls. These border controls were a clear violation of the U.S. Constitution granting the sole authority to regulate interstate commerce to the federal government. However, due to the Senate's inability to agree on new Supreme Court justices, the Court was down to only four members, too few to allow cases to be heard after a recent law passed by Congress. It was one of the few laws the broken Congress had approved. Even the staunchest political opponents didn't want the Court interfering in their fights. Therefore, there was no current legal challenge to the state border patrols being considered by the high Court.

"Carol, there's the Pennsylvania border, and we're right on time. Here we go."

Four booths – similar to toll booths – stretched across the southbound highway that was now divided into four lanes. Each booth commanded a lane that was blocked by a gate. Tony headed for the right-most gate. Tony slowed the Subaru to a modest pace so as not to attract attention. Closer and closer they approached the gate with no sign of any guards. "Open, open," Tony uttered under his breath. He glanced at Carol out of the corner of his right eye. Both her hands were clutched into fists and were moving slowly up and down as if she was cheering for a touchdown by her beloved Buffalo Bills.

They were now inches from the gate. The gate slowly rose. Jason had come through on his promise.

"Tony, we made it." Carol was jumping up and down with joy in her seat.

Tony cautiously accelerated as they passed through the gate. Twenty yards from the gate he brought the Forrester back to normal speed.

"We did it, we did it." Carol was happier than she'd been in months. She reached over and gave Tony a quick kiss on his cheek.

Then there were three sharp sounds - bang, bang, bang.

"Tony, they're shooting at us."

"Carol, get your head down." Tony did the same and steered with one eye looking over the steering wheel. He pushed the accelerator to the floor.

Then there was the horrible sound of breaking glass. "Carol, we've been hit. Are you OK? Say something."

CHAPTER 6

The Capitol, Washington DC, Monday, January 3, Early Evening

MARK LOOKED AT HIS WATCH. 7:00 PM. DENISE'S FRIEND DARLENE, who worked for the late Senator Cooley, was supposed to meet them at Cooley's office at 7. Mark wondered if he had made the right decision. He could just see the headlines now: 'South Carolina Senator Arrested for Breaking and Entering Deceased Colleague's Office.' Although it might take them a few days, Denise assured Mark the Capitol Police would eventually close off Bee's office. If Mark wanted to look at Cooley's files, it was likely now or never.

Hurrying around the corner of the hallway appeared a woman Mark assumed was Darlene. She was surprisingly similar in stature and looks to Denise. Maybe 5'4", early 40ish, attractive but not glamorous, gray-brown hair, and curvy. It was almost like Denise and Darlene were twins. Mischievously Mark thought they could be referred to as the 'Double D twins,' with 'Double D' carrying a dual meaning. Of course, political correctness would never permit it.

Denise and Darlene hugged. "Senator Williams, this is Darlene Huggins. She does, I mean, did, the same things for Senator Cooley as I do for you." "Senator Williams, it's a pleasure to meet you," Darlene stated as she held out her hand.

That voice, Mark thought to himself, it's almost exactly the same as Denise's. Mark took Darlene's hand with a polite shake. "Your voice is very similar to Denise's. Are you also from the Upstate?"

Darlene seemed puzzled and turned to look at Denise.

"He means Upstate South Carolina." Without giving Darlene an opening to answer, Denise continued. "Yes, we're both from the Upstate. In fact, we knew each other in school. But after college, life took us to different directions, and Darlene ended up in North Carolina. Right, Darlene?"

"Oh, yes, right." I moved around North Carolina a lot going from job to job before I ended up with Senator Cooley. What a great person. I just can't believe she's gone." Darlene started to choke up.

Denise embraced Darlene and patted her on the back. "There, there, we'll all miss Senator Cooley. Which is why we want to find out who killed her."

"We don't know for sure Senator Cooley was murdered," corrected Mark. "I know we have our strong suspicions, but we'll have to wait for the autopsy results for a firm answer."

"I worked for Senator Cooley for eight years," added a now-composed Darlene. "For her age – no, let me revise that – for any age, she was super fit. She went to the Capitol gym almost every day. She was a big fan of the stair master. She also watched what she ate. Her only vice that I know of was a fondness for liquor, mainly vodka. But many studies say a little booze each day is good for you."

Mark worried that Denise and Darlene – the 'twins' – could chatter on all night. Even though the Capitol was under-staffed and under-protected, there was still a chance a night guard would discover them.

"Darlene, I know Denise filled you in, but to recap, just before she died, Senator Cooley whispered to me, 'get the files.' I don't know if she meant computer files or paper files, if she had any. Can you help us?"

"I sure can, and I want to. If someone killed Senator Cooley, I want them found."

Darlene unlocked Cooley's office door, flicked on the lights, and took them in to Cooley's private office.

"Darlene, don't you think we should keep the lights off? Worried Mark. He reached into his jacket pocket. "I brought along three small, but powerful, flashlights."

Darlene waved him off. "No, don't worry Senator Williams. There are people in these offices at all hours. If anyone comes by, I can handle them. Plus, as long as there's no police tape, we have a perfect right to be here." This made sense to Mark.

"Now, I keep digital files for Senator Cooley, and they're out there in my office. But Senator Cooley still liked to keep some paper files, and they're right here in this metal filing cabinet." Darlene pointed to an ugly, drab army green colored, rickety four-drawer metal relic. "Senator Williams, I recommend you look through the paper files. There really aren't a lot of them, but Senator Cooley kept them close by, so maybe they're really important. Denise and I will look at the computer files. In fact, we can each work at a separate monitor and split the work."

"Is there anything special we should be looking for?" asked Denise.

Mark frowned. "I wish I knew. I guess anything that is very negative toward Senator Cooley, especially if it suggests or implies some kind of action against the Senator. Certainly pull any file that communicates an explicit threat to the Senator, although I hope she would have brought that to the attention of law enforcement."

Denise shook her head. "With today's limitations on budgets and personnel, you never know."

The trio moved to their respective spaces, with Denise and Darlene at separate computers in the outer office and Mark in Bee's private office. There was only one desk in the space - Bee's – and Mark felt funny using it, but he had no choice. There were framed pictures of Bee's two adult children, and several family photos dominated by – what Mark assumed to be – grandchildren. On the desk's edges were a couple of pictures of Bee with former and current Presidents. Interestingly, there were no pictures of a husband. Maybe he was deceased, or perhaps Bee was divorced.

Fortunately, paper files occupied only two of the four filing cabinet drawers. Unfortunately, as far as Mark could tell, the files weren't in any special order. He therefore had to look at each one individually.

Many were personal correspondence from supporters who must have meant a lot to Bee. Some were newspaper clippings, such as the one commemorating Beatrice Cooley Day in Maxton, North Carolina, her hometown. Another described the erection of a sign designating a stretch of I-40 for 'Senator Beatrice Cooley.' Bee shared this honor with basketball's Michael Jordan in having the sign put up while the honoree was still alive!

After an hour Mark got up, stretched, and walked to the outer office to see how the twins were doing.

Both looked to be diligently at work. "Found anything interesting?"

Darlene spoke for the twins. "Not really. Just normal correspondence with constituents, mayors and commissioners, governors, and other senators. I told Denise I wasn't hopeful we'd find anything since I see all these letters when they come in."

"Same for me," agreed Mark. "I have a few more files to go and that's it. Maybe Bee – er – Senator Cooley - just didn't know what she was saying."

Back in Bee's office, Mark was relieved for two reasons. First, he was almost done, and second, security hadn't come by to ask what he and the twins were doing. Mark still felt guilty going through Bee's private materials.

Mark's relief was quickly replaced by surprise. Staring at him from the file was maybe the reason – no, likely the reason – for Bee's death – no, murder!

CHAPTER 7

Pennsylvania, Monday, January 3, Early Evening

Carol's voice quivered with fear. "Tony, I don't think I've been hit. At least I don't feel anything. Are you OK?"

"I'm fine." The speedometer showed 90. Fortunately, the road was deserted as the border controls had almost stopped interstate travel. That still didn't prevent Tony from sneaking glances into the rear-view mirror to see if vehicle lights were chasing them. There were none. Maybe the patrol just wanted to scare them. Maybe Jason convinced them not to follow his friends. Or maybe they weren't allowed to pursue violators into Pennsylvania. Who knew what laws were enforced today.

Tony tried to calm Carol. "OK, OK, I think we're good. I don't feel any pain or see any blood. Of course, who can see in this dark?" The last sentence Tony said in a joking way, hoping to elicit a laugh from Carol. None came, so Tony went back to worry. "You're fine, right?"

Tony could now hear Carol crying. Carol was a strong-willed, fearless person, but when those she loved were harmed or in trouble, she could become very emotional.

"Yes," sniffle, "I'm fine. "You know I hate guns, especially when they're pointed at me."

Despite the sniffles, Tony could detect a little levity in Carol's response. He felt better.

"Well, look at it this way. We survived the biggest obstacle. It should be smooth sailing from here. If we drive straight through we'll be in Raleigh before dawn tomorrow. We've got the road to ourselves. I'll drive for a couple more hours and then turn it over to you. So why don't you try to sleep a bit."

"You're right, as you usually are on logical issues." Carol let herself smile. She was a typical emotional Pisces fish, while Tony was the logical Capricorn goat. Although different personalities, they shared a strong work ethic, continuous goal-setting, and stubbornness. So far, the combination had made for a successful marriage.

As Carol turned on her side and wrapped the Afghan around her, Tony's brain visualized their future. He saw them in a quaint bungalow in Raleigh, maybe in the historic neighborhood of Oakwood where their friends lived. Carol would be teaching at one of the local colleges or universities. Any institution would be lucky to have her. Carol had a unique ability to make historical events relevant to today's society. He would be at one of Raleigh's big tech firms, maybe in the famed Research Triangle Park. The region was known for college basketball, so they would become avid fans of N.C. State, UNC, or Duke. And yes, kids were wanted, so maybe they'd have the first of the three they planned.

Tony was brought back to the present with two sightings. The stretch of Pennsylvania they were passing used to be known as 'warehouse row' for the scores of multi-acre product warehouses that served the Northeast. But no more. Like New York, Pennsylvania had implemented disastrous central planning and price controls. Most of the warehouses had now moved to the Southeast, moves that eventually prompted the Keystone state to join New York and close its borders.

Next were the exit signs for the Gettysburg National Battlefield. Tony remembered his first visit to the grounds with his father years ago. He still got chills thinking about the intense three-day fight that most experts said was the turning point of the war in favor of the Union forces. Tony found it ironic that over 165 years ago more than 600,000 Americans lost their lives to preserve the Union. Now it seemed millions were trying to break it apart.

Without warning the Forrester's engine sputtered. Initially Tony wasn't worried, thinking maybe the vehicle just needed a rest. After all, it was old and more than 200,000 miles showed on the odometer. But then the sputtering got louder and the vehicle began jerking back and forth.

Carol woke up. "Tony, what's wrong? Do we need gas?"

Tony was confused. "No, we had a full tank when we left that should take us to Virginia. I didn't want to risk stopping in Pennsylvania or even Maryland for fear the cops have been alerted to our escape." Tony took some pride in realizing they were fugitives from the law – at least from the law in New York. To a 'by the book' Capricorn, this was exciting.

Then the Forrester just stopped. Fortunately there was enough momentum to ease the vehicle to the road's shoulder. Tony tried the ignition several times. Nothing.

Tony pushed the button to pop the hood. Carol looked surprised. "What are you doing? You don't know anything about engines."

"I know. But maybe I can spot a loose wire or something."

"Well, then, you might need this." Carol handed him a small flashlight she always kept in her purse.

Tony shined the light all around the quiet engine but saw nothing that was obviously wrong. Now outside in the brisk evening winter air, Tony thought he smelled something. He walked around to the back of the vehicle and then immediately spied the problem.

"Carol, come here a minute." Carol got out of the Forrester and walked to the trunk.

"Smell that?" asked Tony.

Carol shuck her head yes. "What is it?"

"It's gas." See the trail it left behind us. We've been losing gas for miles. Are here's the reason." Tony pointed to several holes on the right rear of the Subaru.

"Are those bullet holes?"

"You bet. A couple of shots fired by the border patrol guys must have hit the car here and then travelled on to the gas tank. At least we weren't hit. But our gas tank is empty."

Carol thought for a moment. "Can we fix it? Can we maybe put some strong masking tape over the holes? I think there's some in the trunk."

"I'm afraid with all the bouncing and shifting of the car, the tape wouldn't hold. Plus, where are we going to get gas?"

Emotions began to overcome Carol again. "Tony, I'm scared," her voice cracked. "What are we going to do?" "It's night, totally dark, no one is around, we don't have a car, and we have very little money. Let's call your Dad. He'll know what to do."

Tony grabbed Carol by her shoulders. "Carol, look at me. He wouldn't make it through the border. The border goons are probably on high alert after our getaway." Tony thought for a moment before continuing. "Here's what we'll do. We'll gather together only the essentials, stuff them in the two suitcases, and hike ahead. There's got to be a turn-off not too far away with a gas station nearby. We'll get something to eat, rest, and then try to get a ride with someone who's headed south. Maybe we can hitch a ride all the way to Virginia, or even North Carolina."

"But what about the favorite painting my Mom did and the end table your Dad built? Those are the only mementoes we have. Everything else we had to leave in Schenectady." Tears were now streaming down Carol's face.

Tony pulled Carol to him and rubbed her back. "I know, I know. But we have do it. It's our dream. To live, work, and raise our kids in a place where we have freedom and opportunity. We have to be strong and continue moving."

Tony could always reason with Carol and calm her. This time was no different. With their objective set, the two goal-driven individuals quickly repacked the suitcases. Wanting to leave no easy trace of who the Subaru belonged to, Tony removed both license plates and stuffed them in a suitcase. After consuming power bars and gulping the rest of the coffee, the pair bundled up and began walking south.

Thankfully, in what felt like ten miles but was actually only three, an exit led them directly to a 24-hour Sheets. It was now after 9 pm but the lights were still on. Sheets was the jackpot for the weary and worried travelers. Essentially a mini-market with a gas station attached, Sheets offered packaged and prepared food, reasonably clean restrooms, household products, and even clothes. Tony and Carol took turns using the restrooms, then splurged on freshly cooked eggs, bacon, toast, and hot coffee. The server raised an eyebrow upon seeing their suitcases, but said nothing.

Faces washed, bodily functions met, and their stomachs full, Tony and Carol plotted their next moves.

The logical Tony started. "We obviously need to hitch a ride to at least Virginia. We can offer money. We have almost all the $2000 in cash we brought."

People-person Carol added. "We just can't approach anyone. An older couple who might be driving to Florida to escape the northern winter would be perfect. We might remind them of the grandkids."

"Here's a problem, however," cautioned Tony. "Although I hope not, there's a possibility we might have to pass border guards at the Pennsylvania/Maryland line who may have been alerted to be on the lookout for two people just like you and me. I think a better target would be a professional truck driver in one of those big 18-wheelers with a sleeping area behind the cab. That would make a perfect hiding place. Plus, the driver would have permits allowing him to cross state lines."

Carol grinned. "I recently read an academic paper comparing today's long-haul truck drivers to the merchant marine sea captains of the 18th century. Both have a deep independent streak and seek out adventure. Those are the perfect characteristics motivating a person to take pity on us and flout the law."

"Bingo," Tony cheerily announced. "Then we'll look for an 18-wheeler with a sleeping compartment going south. We'll both have to turn on the charm and convince him, or maybe her," Tony said a twinkle, "of the honor and worth of this mission of mercy."

Carol rolled her eyes. "If it's charm we need, then move over, that's my department."

"That's right, you charmed me!"

Carol and Tony tried to be inconspicuous as they waited outside with their suitcases while carefully examining all comers and goers. They kept particular attention on the diesel pumps, since that's where the 18-wheelers would head.

After about a half hour, one of the behemoths arrived. The driver got out, started the gas pump, and then strolled to the store.

Carol approached her mark. "Excuse me sir, are you headed south?"

Clearly giving the once-over to Carol – even though an annoyed Tony was nearby - the driver replied. "I wish I was, little lady, but no, I'm going to Syracuse. Too bad for both of us."

Good, thought Tony. Upon returning, Carol indicated she enjoyed the encounter by saying to Tony, "I kind of like being eye-candy."

Fifteen minutes later another 18-wheeler approached. The driver walked with a limp, seemed to be in his 60s, and had a pleasant looking face.

"Excuse me sir, I hate to bother you, but we're sort of in a jam." Carol pointed to Tony, who smiled. "By any chance are you driving south?"

The driver seemed to enjoy being approached. He stopped, removed his hat, smiled, and said, "Yes I am. Can I be of some help?"

Carol and Tony's eyes met with looks that read, 'maybe we're on our way.'

"Are you going to Virginia or even further south?"

"No, my last stop is a warehouse in Washington."

CHAPTER 8

Phoenix Arizona, Monday, January 3, Early Evening

MARIA HAD BEEN DREAMING OF THE FAMILY DINNER FOR MONTHS, long before the election made her daughter, Theresa, the Governor. With the passing of Eugenio, Maria was now head of the family. She made it clear to Theresa that on the day of her inauguration, her daughter's first meal as Governor would not be with fat-cat contributors or pompous politicians. No, it would be with Theresa's family. Even a Governor's powers are limited, especially a Governor who loves her mother. Theresa turned down many invitations to be with her family.

As Theresa was being driven – another perk of being Governor – by her Arizona State Police detail specifically charged with guarding her at all times, she hoped the dinner would be without another family fight. Her brothers, Luis and Armando, although U.S citizens by birth, had been seduced by the idea of reviving the Mexican Empire. The dream of an expanded Mexico including much of the western U.S. was being fueled by the wealthy Arizona businessman Richard Fuentes, who insisted on being called 'El Ricardo.' Fuentes made his money by developing and marketing a beer, Revivo, which targeted Hispanic Americans in several states. Revivo had even penetrated the Mexican market. Having become financially successfully – although many thought his success was vastly overstated - it was thought Fuentes was looking for wider glory. Fuentes argued Mexico was cheated out of the western U.S. lands after the Mexican-American

War in the 19th century, and it was he – El Ricardo – who would right that wrong.

Most people didn't take Fuentes seriously. After all, he was born in the U.S. and didn't even speak Spanish. Many saw his push for a new Mexican Empire as just an advertising stunt to keep his name in the news. Fuentes's political action committee, the Mexico Rising Fund, made some political donations, but most politicians, including Theresa, kept Fuentes and his money at arm's length. Some crackpots thought Fuentes was a mouthpiece for the Mexican government. Most reasonable people, including those in the Mexican government, knew this was absurd.

Regardless of Fuentes' real motives, he had captured the attention of numerous young people of Hispanic heritage. Theresa thought this was the real danger of Fuentes – diverting the focus of impressionable youths away from constructive activities that would ultimately get them ahead in life. Unfortunately for Theresa's family, two of those youths who were clinging to Fuentes' vision were Luis and Armando.

Maria hugged and kissed Theresa as she entered the modest, yet well-kept and inviting home. The kitchen was the hub of life in close-knit Mexican families. Although not massive like the kitchens of many new-built homes, the room's arrangement immediately indicated its use by an experienced cook. The refrigerator-sink-stove triangle provided for efficient use of the modest space. And while not modern, the appliances were clearly well cared for, even giving off a glow from the afternoon light. Theresa had many good years growing up in this house.

"Theresa, where's your manners. I don't care that you're the Governor. Invite your *guardias* (guards) in for dinner," commanded Maria.

"*Madre* (Mother), they're not allowed in. They have to be outside to constantly surveille the area for potential threats."

"Threats, what threats," huffed Maria. "This neighborhood has always been safe during the thirty years I've lived here, twenty-five of them with your father, bless his soul. But Madam Governor, can I at least take them some food?"

"Yes, my constituent," answered Theresa with a wink. "You have my permission to feed the guards." Maria beamed as she gathered together plates of homemade tacos, refried beans, and southwest salad.

Theresa moved into the small den where her brothers and cousin were engaged in conversation. She noticed the arrangement of family pictures had been altered on the wall surrounding the fireplace. In the past Maria was careful to have equal numbers of photos of her three children on the wall. Now, a number of the pictures of Luis and Armando had been replaced by those of Theresa. Theresa made a mental note to speak to Maria about this.

Theresa greeted her cousin Sophia first. They were similar in age, and Theresa had always treated Sophia like the sister she never had. Sophia's parents, now deceased, had emigrated to the U.S. with Sophia legally and had ultimately become citizens. So had Sophia. In the past there had been some friction between Theresa's brothers and Sophia, with the brothers referring to Sophia as a 'gringo' because she willingly sought U.S. citizenship. Of course, the brothers were also U.S. citizens due to their being born in the country, but they claimed this was different because they had no control over their birthplace.

"Should I bow and call you 'Her Excellency'?" Luis only half-teasingly asked.

"Yes, you should call me 'Her Excellency,' but not because I'm Governor, but because of all the crap I had to put up with growing up with you." Theresa smiled and gave Luis a big hug to let him know she was joking.

Luis was not amused. "Crap – wow – are big shot Governors allowed to say that word? Isn't it banned along with 'Hispanic', 'Mexican Empire', and 'El Ricardo'"?

"Play nice and show a little respect," shot back Sophia, a well-respected and well-compensated divorce attorney who was used to family squabbles.

"Shut up gringo," hissed Luis. "Since you've got yours, you don't care about our country. And in case you've forgotten – which I know you have – 'our country' means Mexico and the rightful Mexican Empire."

Armando was the middle child, the natural peacemaker, who while agreeing with his little brother, didn't always like his tactics. "Luis, that's enough. We're here today to celebrate what our sister has accomplished. There'll be plenty of time to discuss the future of our two countries, Mexico and the United States, with our new Governor."

"I need a beer." Luis started for the kitchen.

Armando grabbed Luis' arm. "Not before you apologize to both Theresa and Sophia."

With his head down and positioned in the direction of both Sophia and Theresa, Luis muttered a soft "I'm sorry."

"That's not good enough," ordered Armando.

Looking up with watery eyes and using a much more serious tone, Luis relented, "Sophia and Theresa, I really am sorry. You know I love both of you. But you know I get very passionate about the things I believe in. I just have to learn how to control that passion, and I will, believe me."

Luis, Sophia, and Theresa had a group hug before Luis departed for the kitchen.

Theresa broke the silence and looked seriously at Armando. "Do the two of you really believe what Fuentes is pushing?" Without waiting for an answer, she continued. "Why would you? We can certainly honor and respect our heritage. I do, and Sophia does. I have friends from many other backgrounds – German, Irish, English, and, of course, African – and they celebrate their cultures. One colleague at the engineering firm was 6th generation English, had never set foot in England, yet he purposefully spoke with an English accent. But we're all Americans, especially you two and Luis with your citizenship. I'm not that lucky, but at least I'm accepted and I hope respected. If not, why was I elected Governor?"

"I guess, Sis, you are respected by the – what – 55% who voted for you. But what about the 45% who voted for the other candidates? I bet a lot of them don't respect you and want you to go back to

Mexico. Just look at how Americans don't respect our names. They always have to change them. At work, most people call me 'Arnie', not Armando. And Luis is usually called Lewis, or Lou. They can't even honor us by using our real names."

"Wait a minute," countered Sophia. "That's just the American thing to do – shorten everything. It's done for all names. A partner at the law firm has a beautiful name, Michelle. You know what everyone – including me – calls her? Shel. That's right, Michelle is shortened to Shel. Robert is Bob, Jonathan is John, and Elizabeth is Liz. It's just the way we Americans are. We're always in a hurry, even in our speaking."

"Many of my friends refer to me as 'The,'" Theresa added. "Of course, now they'll have to call me 'The Governor.' Get it – '*The* Governor,' since there's only one governor at a time."

Armando initially looked confused, but then finally cracked a smile. In contrast, Sophia doubled over laughing.

Theresa then became very serious. "I'll be honest with you. As a state senator, I finessed this issue of how much we owe to the country of our background and how much we owe to our adopted country. But in the weeks between the election and my inauguration today, I've given the question much thought. Here's what I think. Whether we were born here, were brought here, or sneaked in here, this – the United State of America – is our country. And if it's a question of breaking up the country to form a Mexican Empire, or some kind of state association, versus keeping the Union intact, I'm for the Union. I swore to that. I also know our Union - our country - has many issues and is far from perfect. Yet it has made progress. Blatant discrimination has dropped while tolerance has risen. New technology developed in recent decades has made health care more accessible and affordable. Virtualization is allowing more people the option to work from home, thus limiting commuting, reducing pollution, and allowing for increased parental time with children. And the development of ecological preserves and environmentally-friendly tourism in Central America has given a real economic boost to the people of the region and has cut their incentive to migrate to the U.S."

Maria came into the den. Seeing her, Theresa apologized. "Sorry, Momma, we got to talking and forgot to help you set the table. We'll help now."

Looking distressed, Maria replied, "Theresa, one of your guards needs to talk to you. He says it's urgent."

Leaving the den, Theresa found Sgt. Wayne Burrell, the head of her security detail, standing just inside the kitchen door to the porch. She noticed some taco stains on his shirt.

"Must have been good," Theresa smiled, pointing to the stains.

Burrell grinned slightly, but was all business. "Governor, we just learned of some disturbing news."

Theresa braced herself – terrorist attack, power outage, natural disaster – her mind quickly flipped through the possibilities.

"What is it, Sgt. Burrell?"

"Madam Governor, I don't exactly know what it means. We've been informed the federal government just defaulted on the national debt."

CHAPTER 9

The Capitol, Washington, DC, Monday, January 3, Late Evening

Still worried that security might find them, Mark, Denise, and Darlene took the document to Mark's office. Mark's stomach was tight and his palms sweaty the entire way. The twins appeared calm and actually excited.

Once in the office, Darlene couldn't contain her interest. "Senator, what's in that document? We didn't find anything remotely suspicious on the computers." Denise had to chime in, "We really didn't."

The three were gathered around Mark's desk. While it appeared to be gossip for the twins, it was serious and potential political dynamite for Mark.

"This document looks to be a report from the British Intelligence Agency MI6." Mark pointed to the letterhead as the twins peered over his shoulders. "The agent talks about a possible plot by the Mexican government to generate support in the U.S. for a constitutional convention, and to ultimately take back land in the western part of the country, including California."

Denise looked confused. "I don't understand. What's a constitutional convention, and why would Mexico want us to have one?"

Mark explained the meaning of a constitutional convention, what it could mean, and how the Concon movement was working to make it happen.

Darlene spoke up. "Let me get this straight. The Concon group essentially wants to destroy the country. That's horrible. The leaders should be tracked down and put in prison. But why would this involve Senator Cooley?"

Mark didn't think this was the time to teach Darlene about the concept of freedom of speech and freedom of assembly, no matter how much he thought Concon was wrong. That was a topic for another day. But he was surprised Darlene wasn't aware of Bee's strong opposition to Concon's objectives.

"You didn't know Senator Cooley was one of the leaders of the opponents to Concon? I would have expected she had you type some correspondence indicating her views about the movement."

Darlene appeared defensive and uncertain of how to answer Mark's question. "Uh, no, I don't remember typing anything about any Concon. Of course, when I type, I focus on spelling and punctuation and not necessarily the meaning of the words."

Denise quickly jumped in. "Senator, are you against Concon?

Mark thought this was an odd question especially at this time, but he answered it honestly. "Yes I am, especially after I tell you what else is in the document."

"There's more," added Darlene. "This is getting juicy." Mark didn't smile.

"Yes, there is, and it's even more troubling. According to the report, an alliance between France and Spain is the real power behind Mexico's actions. The report speculates France and Spain see big economic opportunities if they help establish a new Mexican Empire that includes a large part of the United States. They'd be able to tap into the region's massive energy resources in Texas, the Dakotas, and the Gulf, as well as into what's left of the tech and entertainment industries in California.

"That reminds me of the Bourbon dynasty in the 16th and 17th centuries," interjected Darlene.

Mark was stunned by Darlene's comment. "You know about the Bourbon dynasty?"

"Oh sure. I was a European history major in college. The Bourbons were fascinating. I just loved their clothes, arranged marriages, and wealth. They were on the thrones of both France and Spain when the two countries combined their forces to flight England. In fact, if it wasn't for the Bourbons helping the American colonists, there may never have been a United States."

Although he was surprised at the source, Darlene's comments made sense to Mark. With the European Union long dissolved, the former members had rushed to form new alliances. Germany, Poland, and Ukraine established an eastern common market. The United Kingdom created commercial ties to traditional allies in Scandinavia and with Belgium and the Netherlands on the continent. Putting aside centuries of suspicion, there now was an association of the Balkan countries. Only Italy could find no takers for an alliance, mainly because the Italians couldn't even agree among themselves, let alone with other countries. Therefore, it was not surprising France and Spain had renewed their bonds.

"Senator, what does this mean? What should we do? Who should we tell?" Denise asked in rapid succession.

"I don't know yet. I need to think before I decide. But I do know one thing. Important people need to know about this document."

Denise and Darlene looked at each other.

Mark remained at his desk. He thought his first day as a U.S. Senator would be exciting and thrilling, but he never thought it would be like this. First he was inaugurated. Then he was confronted by the appalling condition of the Capitol and his office. He was introduced to one of the most esteemed Senators of the day, only to have her die in his office, likely the result of foul play. To top off the day, he illegally broke into another Senator's office only to find a plot by foreign powers to break up the United States.

A growl from his stomach reminded Mark he hadn't eaten since breakfast. He also hadn't communicated with Cheryl since muting his cell phone when Bee arrived. Sure enough, there were several calls from Cheryl. Mark unmuted the phone and began to call Cheryl to - ....

Then the office lights went out. Then Mark's lights went out.

CHAPTER 10

Pennsylvania, Monday, January 3, Late Evening

"You two remind me of my grandkids." Doug Peterson looked somewhat wistfully at Carol and Tony. His driving schedule often left little time for his grandchildren. After a twenty-year hitch in the Army, Doug had driven for a variety of trucking firms for twenty-two years. He planned to retire in three years when he could finally collect his full Social Security.

"That's so nice of you to say, Mr. Peterson." Carol genuinely meant it. In just a few minutes, she and Tony had formed an affection for Doug Peterson, so much so that they were willing to entrust their lives with him. They told Doug about their plans, and he had agreed to take them to Washington, but that was as far as he could go. After delivering his load to a warehouse, he would immediately pick up another and return to Buffalo. He also agreed to allow Carol and Tony to ride in the sleeping quarters in the rear of the cab. He wouldn't be using the cot during the 'quick' up and back 16- hour run, even though federal regulations required it.

"I get it you kids want to start a better life in the South. New York has become unlivable. Everyone would have eventually left if the state government hadn't funded those border guards. They're just thugs acting like police. They're a disgrace. I bet if I came at them with my old M16 rifle they'd all run."

After Doug had offered them a ride, Carol and Tony had to make a quick decision. Doug seemed honest, and, truthfully, the couple had no other immediate options. All they could do is wait for more truckers, but that too was dangerous. There was always the possibility someone would report them to the New York or Pennsylvania police.

Carol was first to climb in to the cab and then up to the sleeping quarters, followed by Tony. "It's amazing how large and cozy this area is." Carol lied, but she wanted to make Doug feel good.

"It's not bad," answered Doug. "Not as good as my bed at home, but better than what I had in 1991 during the Persian Gulf War."

Tony grimaced as he pulled his leg onto the cot, being careful not to kick Carol in the face. "Yea, my Dad was there too. You two probably didn't cross paths. He was in a quartermaster unit. Never shot anything, unless you count rats trying to get at the food."

Doug laughed. "Hey, don't count out your Dad. None of us could have done anything without the quartermasters. They kept us fed, bivouacked, and – most important of all – supplied with ammunition. Nothing happens without the supply guys."

Carol and Tony finally situated themselves, lying side by side across the length of the cot. The cot was thin and lumpy, but at least they could stretch out their legs.

"When we get going, I want you to pull those blankets completely over yourselves, leaving the extra in front. Make it look messy. That way, if there are guards at the Pennsylvania-Maryland border and they look inside the cab, they'll think I just left a cot with messy blankets."

Carol and Tony didn't know how much farther back they could push themselves, but they'd try.

The 18-wheeler was diesel powered, so it was never fully turned off. After climbing into his position in the driver's seat, Doug pushed some buttons to bring the engine back from sleeping mode. When fully awake, the engine's noise was loud and powerful but rhythmic.

"Here we go kids. It'll be about a three-hour drive to DC," yelled Doug.

After only a few minutes, Carol pulled back the covers. "Say Mr. Peterson, we never asked you what you're hauling." Carol was inquisitive about everything.

"Lamps. I think about 400 of them. Taking them from a factory outside of Buffalo to a warehouse in DC. They're from one of the few remaining lamp factories in the country. The company is probably sorry they didn't get out before New York clamped down. After dropping off the lamps I'm taking a return shipment of soap from another warehouse back to Buffalo. At least if I get stranded, I'll be clean." Doug laughed at his own joke.

Despite the cramped quarters, Carol and Tony were so tired they both feel sound asleep. Doug thought so when he shouted back some questions with no response. He smiled when he remembered himself at their age. Graduating from high school in Endicott, New York, he felt the country was at his fingertips. He could go anywhere and do anything. Life was exciting. He wanted to see the world, so he joined the Army, liked it, and stayed in. But when he returned to Endicott after retiring from the Army, life had changed. It seemed young people grew up afraid and unsure of themselves. They were apprehensive about the future rather than chomping at the bit to see what was ahead. And the State made it worse with its micro-management of the economy and now their controls on who could leave the state. In many ways Doug was glad he was 62 rather than 32 like Carol and Tony. But unlike many of their contemporaries, at least Carol and Tony had hope and guts. Doug would do everything he could to see them succeed.

After an hour Carol woke up. Tony – still asleep – had his body wrapped around hers in a protective, but also sensual, way. With all the time and stress of preparing to move and saying goodbye to their families, Carol and Tony had not made love in over a week, a long time for relative newlyweds. Carol immediately had a strong longing for Tony. A modest person, Carol felt shy about her feelings for Tony since they were only a few feet away from Doug. Still, they were a couple feet higher up and the tall seats in the front of the cab formed a barrier of sorts.

Carol followed her feelings. She turned to face Tony and began undoing his belt and unzipping his pants. Tony awakened and, without hesitation, opened Carol's shirt, removed her bra, and – with her help – began pulling down her jeans. Carol whispered in Tony's ear that they needed to be quiet, and Tony nodded.

It was the most intense and satisfying love-making of their young marriage. Maybe it was a celebration of their escape from New York or anticipation of a better life ahead. Before she and Tony drifted off to sleep again, Carol wondered how ironic it would be if they had just conceived their first child.

Up in the driver's seat, Doug knew what had happened and smiled. Oh, to be young again, he thought.

The remaining time passed uneventfully. The 18-wheeler was now about 20 miles from the Pennsylvania-Maryland line on I-83. This was a different, more travelled route than Carol and Tony had planned to take to avoid the possibility of border guards. But Doug had a deadline to meet, so he had no choice but to use the most direct route to Washington. Doug would have bet a week's pay there would be Pennsylvania border guards at the crossing. He thought about leaving Carol and Tony sleep, but then decided that wouldn't be a good idea if the guards started poking around in the cab. If Carol or Tony were like him, one of them might wake up with a loud "huh."

"OK sleepy heads, time to wake up. We're not far from Maryland." Carol stirred, making sure her shirt was buttoned and her pants zipped. Tony did the same. Carol cautiously poked her head out from under the blankets. "Doug, do you think this will work?

"We can only hope. Just make sure the area looks like I'm a sloppy housekeeper. I really don't see any reason why the guards will look back there. It's certainly not easy to get to."

Carol and Tony did the best they could to make the sleeping loft look natural, albeit sloppy. Under the covers they felt a little uneasy as they couldn't see what was happening. But Doug gave them a running commentary.

"OK, here we are at the border and, as I expected, there is a checkpoint. I'm easing over to the far right lane to stay away from as many guards as possible."

At the sight of the 18-wheeler, two guards approached and waved Doug over to a parking area away from the gate.

"Oh, oh, I wonder what this means."

The first guard, an overweight male in his early thirties, walked over to the cab as Doug stopped. His partner, a slightly older but also heavy-set male, hung back. Both guards were armed with pistols.

"You're good right there. OK, step out of the cab."

Doug did as he said. "Something wrong officer?"

"We need to check your cargo and make sure no one is hiding in there." The second guard had now joined the first and walked with Doug to the rear of the 18-wheeler.

"I just have a load of lamps, 400 to be exact." Doug put on a fake smile for the two men he already despised.

Doug opened the two swinging doors to the 18-wheeler's trailer.

"Wow, that's a lot of boxes," observed the older guard. "You know you're going to have to unload all of them, open them, and let us make sure they're really lamps."

"What! That'll take hours, and I'm on a schedule. Can't you just look at a few and then let me get on my way?"

"No way, Pops, we've got to be sure you're not in the people-smuggling business. You'd be surprised what people will do to move out of our great state."

Doug thought about saying, yeah, leaving only bozos like you, but he knew that wouldn't help.

The younger guard spoke up. "You know, there is a way we can let you go without inspecting all the boxes."

"There is." Doug felt relieved.

"Yeah. I'm sure whoever is getting these lamps won't miss a few. You can always say they were broken in shipment." The guard laughed, with his partner soon joining in.

"That's right," added the older guard, looking at his partner. "Doesn't your girlfriend need a couple of lamps in her new apartment?"

"She sure does, and I bet these would be perfect."

Inwardly Doug steamed. He wanted to take both of these fatsos out, and he could, even though they were half his age. Yet he knew what was going on, and he had to play along. Trying hard not to grit his teeth, Doug agreed.

"Sure, what two, maybe three boxes could be counted as damaged. Does that sound about right?"

The younger guard gave a snarky smile of nicotine-stained teeth. "You know Pops, you catch on fast. I actually think it's a bargain only three boxes were damaged in delivery. You're a good driver." The guard got a good self-satisfying laugh out of his last comment.

The two guards put three lamp boxes near the curbing of the pavement.

"I know what someone is going to be getting later tonight when he shows up with these lamps," snickered the older guard.

"Can I get on my way now?" Doug asked politely.

"Not so fast, Pops. We still have to inspect the cab."

The guards moved toward the 18-wheeler's cab with Doug trailing. "There's nothing up there except my personal stuff." Doug worked hard to keep from sounding nervous.

"Well, we have to see for ourselves."

The guards first opened the driver's side of the cab, looked in, and then satisfied, moved around the front of the cab to the rider's side. They quickly perused the rider's seat.

"See, all good." Doug moved to close the door.

"Not yet, Pops. I still have to go upstairs." The younger guard pushed the back of the rider's seat forwarded, and then with a lot of straining and puffing, pulled himself up into the sleeping section. "You're a messy sleeper, Pops. Didn't your mommy show you how to make a bed?" Just as the guard's right arm moved to pull back the covers, Carol slammed both her legs into the guard's chest, doubling him over and leaving him gasping for breath. Before the guard could recover, Tony landed his right fist into the guard's left jaw, leaving him to collapse into a blubbery heap.

The older guard reacted slowly, giving Doug time to swing him around, send his left fist into the guard's stomach, and then finish him off with a quick punch to the jaw.

Fortunately, with the 18-wheeler parked on the far right of the crossing complex, all the action was out of sight of the other guards.

Doug pulled the older guard into some weeds alongside the pavement, and Carol and Tony did the same with the younger guard.

"Let's hurry," barked Doug. "Those guys are out now, but they won't be for long."

Carol jumped back into the cab's sleeping area, while Tony took the 'shotgun' seat next to Doug. There was no need to hide now.

Doug revved up the engine and headed for the far right gate, which was down. The fiberglass barrier was no match for the 80,000-pound truck. A short-lived snapping and crumbling sound was all the trio heard.

"We made it. We're free in Maryland." Tony celebrated by high-fiving Doug and turning for a quick kiss with Carol.

"That sure was scary. Those two guys sure were a-holes. Trying to shake me down in order to pass through. And you two." Doug turned to face Tony and catch a glimpse of Carol. "What courage. And what power you have in your legs, Carol. I bet you played some type of sports."

"I did play soccer in high school and some in undergraduate school. All those squats we did in training sure did come in handy."

'I'll wager the Pennsylvania Police jerks won't pursue us. We can settle back and enjoy our final few miles into DC. On the downside, I'll probably have to find a different route back to Buffalo. I imagine I'm not welcome in the Keystone state."

No sooner than Doug's words were out of his mouth than he saw flashing red lights bearing down on the rig from behind.

CHAPTER 11

Maryland, Tuesday, January 4, Early Morning

"WHAT A FOOL I WAS," EXCLAIMED DOUG. "THOSE PENNSYLVANIA goons are chasing us. They're probably pissed because we beat the crap out of them."

Carol and Tony both turned around and saw the red lights of two police cruisers getting closer.

"What can we do? Is there any way we can out-run them?" Carol knew what the answers would be, but she still had to ask.

"No way," answered Doug. This rig can only hit 80 miles per hour, and that's with the peddle hitting the floor. Those police cars have special engines reaching 150."

Doug noticed the two cars splitting. One was staying in back of the 18-wheeler while the other was coming around the left side. Soon it passed him and was speeding ahead.

Tony watched the move. "Where's that one going?"

"I think I know what he's going to do, and it's not good for us. Since it's 2 am and there's no traffic except us and them, the cruiser in the back is going to keep away any traffic that does show up. Once the cruiser in front is far enough ahead, it'll deploy a stop-stick."

"A stop-stick?" asked the ever curious Carol. "What's that?"

"Dad took me to a demonstration of a stop-stick a couple months back," explained Tony. It's a set of interwoven metal barbs laid across a road. When a vehicle crosses them, the barbs puncture the tires, and the tires will slowly deflate. Eventually the vehicle will stop. It's much safer and more effective than shooting out the tires."

"Why can't we just go around it?" asked a hopeful Carol.

"We could try, but the stop-stick can also be laid outside the pavement on the road shoulder or even in grass and weeds," continued Tony.

"And I'd rather jump out of this rig than try to drive it on the shoulder or grass," emphasized Doug.

Carol buried her face in her palms. "It looks like we're sunk. I wish we never started this trip."

Doug pointed ahead, "There they are. Just as I thought. In a few minutes we'll be able to see the stop-stick. I'm going to slow down. I'm sorry kids, but it looks like this is the end of the road." Trying to lighten the mood, Doug added, "That last sentence was a little trucker humor."

Suddenly Doug turned serious. "I don't understand. Where did those other cop cars come from?"

The Pennsylvania guards that deployed the stop-sticks had been joined by five other police vehicles. But instead of the gray colors of the Pennsylvania police, the additional cars were black. Then seeing the distinctive yellow, red, black and white emblem, Doug knew exactly who they were.

"Those are Maryland State Police cars. I guess the Pennsylvania guys called for back-up. Figures – they're such whooshes."

Tony wasn't so sure. "Look at that. The Pennsylvania and Maryland cops are arguing. There's even some pushing and shoving going on. And now look. The Maryland cops are taking up the stop-stick. And now it looks like the Pennsylvania cops are getting in their car and driving away."

Doug removed his cap and scratched his head. "I don't get it."

Doug had brought the 18-wheeler to a halt. The Pennsylvania cruiser that had been ahead now passed on the left side of the rig going back to its partner. Doug thought he saw the driver give him the finger.

An immaculately dressed Maryland state trooper approached Doug's side of the cab.

"Sir, I apologize for the drama. Some of those Penn guys think they rule the world. They have no jurisdiction in Maryland, and as far as we know, you violated no Maryland state laws. So as soon as we move those stop-sticks and our cruisers, you can continue on your way." The trooper tipped his hat and walked back to his partners.

Doug, Carol, and Tony were stupefied. "Well, what do you know?" began Doug. "I thought our goose was cooked. This will be a story I'll share with the other drivers for months."

Tony the analyst had the answer. "Actually this makes sense. Maryland has not closed its borders. It's having the same kind of economic growth as Virginia and the rest of the Southeast and blames idiotic state policies for Pennsylvania and New York's woes."

Doug stirred the slumbering rig's engine and started the last leg of their trip to Washington. Soon they were in the outskirts of the sprawling metropolis that was still asleep.

"You kids need some shuteye. I know a decent but affordable Econolodge just a few minutes from here. I'll pay for your room. I feel really bad I can't take you any farther."

The emotional Carol was getting teary-eyed. "Mr. Peterson, please don't feel badly. You've literally saved our lives, and we'll be forever grateful. Also, we have more than enough to cover the hotel room."

"Well, it's been my pleasure knowing you. Meeting you two makes me much more hopeful for the future of our country. Oh, and once again, it's Doug, not Mr. Peterson. Also, I might add, Douglas is a wonderful name for a child." Doug punctuated his comment with a wink.

Doug pulled the 18-wheeler into the Econolodge and made sure lights were on in the office. After the three climbed out of the rig there were hugs all around.

Before she and Tony headed for the office, Carol had one more question. "Mr. Peterson – I mean, Doug – can I ask one more thing?"

"Of course, anything."

"Tony and I will have to stay in DC for a little bit to replenish our funds so we can buy a car and other things we left behind. You probably talk to a lot of drivers from around here. Have you heard of any companies or maybe government agencies that are hiring? Tony and I are willing to do almost anything."

Doug rubbed his jaw. "Let me think. I know the government isn't hiring because of their money problems. I don't know of anything open in the warehouses I go to. Wait a minute, here's an idea. A buddy delivered some things to the British Embassy over on Massachusetts Avenue. I remember he said there was an entire room used to interview people for jobs because the Brits bought the next-door building and are expanding. So that might be a start."

"That's great, Doug. You've always come through for us. We'll certainly check it out."

For a few minutes Doug just stood looking at Carol and Tony. For a moment they thought he might cry. He didn't, but instead grabbed each of them for a final big embrace. After turning to walk to the truck, he stopped, turned around again, and gave them a thumbs-up. Doug then climbed into the cab and headed out of the parking lot. He waved one last time and even touted the rig's horn.

Carrying their limited luggage, Carol and Tony walked toward the office. "I'll always remember him," Tony mused. "I put him in the same class as my Dad. In fact, I'd like them to meet one day. And you know what, naming one of children Doug is not a bad idea."

"Speaking of children, do you think he knew what we did earlier today in the sleeping loft? You know, when we weren't sleeping?

Tony answered with no hesitation. "Oh yes, he knew, you can be sure of it. That wink confirmed it."

CHAPTER 12

The Capitol, Washington, DC, Tuesday, January 4, Early Morning

Mark was awakened by the ringing of his cell phone. He fumbled for the phone and answered. It was Cheryl.

"Mark, where in the hell have you been. I've been trying to reach you for hours. You haven't been out partying with one of those twinkie secretaries?"

Cheryl did harbor a suspicious streak. Part of it was a result of how she and Mark had aged. Mark had maintained his college weight – when they met – by consistently exercising. His hair had grey flecks and his face had a series of deep wrinkles, but those changes had only made him look more distinguished. In fact, during his Senate campaign, he received several admiring comments and even a couple of proposals for meeting.

When they married Cheryl had natural blond hair, an athletic figure, and was never without offers for dates. After having two children, she now carried about thirty more pounds than during her college days, and along with wrinkles, her face had started to droop. Although their boys had not yet even begun college, several supporters during the campaign asked how many grandchildren she and Mark had. In Cheryl's mind, aging was one of the last vestiges of gender discrimination.

"No, Cheryl, I wasn't partying. I've been out cold for hours since being attacked."

"What! You were attacked." Cheryl's tone immediately turned to concern. "Did that secretary of yours call an ambulance? I'm coming over there right now."

Mark looked at his watch. "Cheryl, it's 3 am. Denise has been gone for hours. I was getting ready to come home when someone must have clobbered me." Mark felt the lump on his head. It hurt.

"I'm good enough to drive and should be home in a few minutes." 'Home' was an efficiency apartment in the nearby Capitol Hill neighborhood. Cheryl had only come to Washington for the inauguration.

"If you say so." There was less sympathy in Cheryl's voice now. "I'm going to try to get some sleep. Remember, I'm driving back to South Carolina today. The boys need at least one of their parents. So be quiet when you come in, although with the cramped size of this place, I'm sure I'll hear you. And if your head still hurts after a few more hours, go see a doctor."

There was no 'love-you' or 'I'll call a doctor right away' from Cheryl. The relationship between Mark and Cheryl had cooled considerably after his entry into politics. Mark wasn't hungry for power. He just thought it was his duty to serve, especially with the track the country had been on in recent decades. Cheryl resented the time public office required from Mark. Unlike some other politicians' spouses who craved the attention, parties, and perks that went along with being an elected official, Cheryl didn't, especially with her consciousness about how she looked.

Mark unlocked the door of the efficiency in twenty minutes. As she promised, Cheryl was sound asleep in the Murphy bed that constituted the bedroom-area of the one-room unit. Mark tip-toed around, put a cold wash cloth on his head, removed his suit, and carefully slid into the bed next to Cheryl. She stirred but did not awaken. Mark was asleep in seconds.

He awoke at 9. Cheryl was gone. He found a note from her on the counter in the kitchenette saying she left at 7 and would call him when she was back home in South Carolina. Again, there was no 'love you.' The only sign of affection – if it could be called that – was a suggestion to see a doctor if he wasn't better.

Fortunately, Mark's head felt much better. He showered, put on clean clothes and a fresh suit, and ate a quick breakfast consisting of a canned protein drink and two pieces of toast. He wished he could hit the gym, but exercise would have to wait. He needed to hurry to the Capitol because committee assignments were being made today.

Back at the office, Denise greeted Mark and noticed a band aid on the back of his head.

"Senator, what happened? Did you fall? Have you had a doctor look at that? Here, sit down and let me get you a cup of coffee."

Mark sat at his desk and gratefully accepted the coffee. He explained to Denise about the assault. Then it struck him. "I haven't checked to see if anything is missing," Mark said out loud. "If I remember correctly, I was looking at the MI6 report we 'retrieved' from Senator Cooley's office. Do you see it?"

Denise looked at Mark's desk as well as around the desk.

"No, I don't. Do you think that's what the guy wanted? And how would he know we had it?"

"Now, I don't know the assailant was a male. I was hit from behind. So it could have been a female. But if we can't find that report, then I think it's a good guess that's what the intruder was after."

Mark glanced at his watch. "Oh, no, look at the time. I've got to hustle to get to the meeting on committee assignments." Mark got up, grabbed his briefcase, and rushed out the door.

"Senator, I'll keep looking for the report and text you if I find anything," Denise shouted as Mark ran down the hallway.

In the old days of two-competing parties, committee assignments were based on two factors – seniority and the importance of the Senator's state. The plumb assignments were foreign affairs, judiciary, finance, and appropriations, and they usually went to Senators with the most years served and Senators from populous states. Those committees received tremendous press coverage and could easily launch a Senator's career to the next level – the Presidency.

The two-party days were gone. With Senators from a dozen parties, power was formed through coalitions. By default, U.S. governance had devolved into a parliamentary system, but the chaotic Italian kind rather than the stable British type. Party alliances in both the Senate and House were constantly falling apart and reforming. Even the Presidency was affected. It had been decades since any presidential candidate received anything close to a majority of the electoral college vote. Indeed, the top vote-getter usually had less than 25% of the total. Typically, and as prescribed by the Constitution, the top three vote-getters in the electoral college were voted on by state delegations in the House of Representatives, with each state having one vote. Again, it took a majority of the states to win, meaning the selection of a President could drag on for months. Once it took almost a year from the time of the election for a President to be named.

Once a President did take office, often she or he often didn't stay long. Impeachment had become a common political weapon. Presidents usually were impeached in their first year of office for almost anything, as was the constitutional prerogative of the House. Four of the last six Presidents had been impeached, convicted, and removed from office.

Mark entered the Senate chamber and immediately saw his fellow Libertarian Senator from Georgia, Joe Ferguson. Ferguson was in his second term and knew the ropes.

"Mark, it's good to see you." Ferguson simultaneously pumped Mark's hand while patting him on the back. "Ready for the circus?"

Mark frowned. "Is it that bad?"

"I'm afraid it is. With coalitions so unstable, one day you might be on the Ag committee, and the next day you'll be off it and be placed on the Intelligence committee."

"I guess this makes it hard to get a lot of work done."

"Work would be a gift here. Mostly we argue with some while embracing others, then the next day we argue with those we had embraced and embrace those we had previously argued with. You really do need a daily scorecard for who's your friend and who's your enemy."

"You heard about Senator Cooley's death?"

Ferguson's face frowned. "I sure did. Great Senator, great person. I heard it happened in your office. Was it a heart attack or a stroke?"

"There's nothing official yet," Mark replied. "But let me ask you this. Concon, the call for new constitutional convention, is it really a big deal?"

"Big deal, that's an understatement. It is 'the' deal in Congress, with committed groups on both sides."

"Is it enough of a big deal to kill for?"

Ferguson's eyes narrowed and he leaned in to Mark's ear. "Yes, it is, so be careful."

After learning he had been appointed to the Agriculture, Aging, Veteran's Affairs, and Administration committees – at least for today - Mark returned to his office. He was surprised to find Lt. Evers waiting in his inner chambers.

"Lt. Evers, are you here to investigate the assault on me?" Mark pointed to his bandaged head. "If so, I'm impressed. Your response time has been considerably improved compared to the time it took you to arrive for Senator Cooley's death."

Evers bristled, but understood. "Despite what you may think, we take attacks of any kind on our elected officials very seriously. We now think the murder of Senator Cooley and the attack on you may be related. As a result, these two cases are receiving my top attention."

"Senator Cooley's death is now officially a murder?" Mark wasn't surprised.

"Yes it is. Senator Cooley was poisoned. The poison was botulinum. It is tasteless and odorless and was probably put in her vodka. Causes the nervous system to shut down immediately. Although we would have liked to have examined the cup Senator Cooley used, as you know, your secretary tossed it in the incinerator." Mark cringed. Denise remained out of sight in her office. "However, my professional opinion is the poison had been added directly to the flask or to the bottle of vodka that was used to fill the flask. I have people at Senator Cooley's apartment right now to find the bottle and look for other clues." Evers paused and looked at his notebook. "Now, give me a full account of the assault on you."

"Well, I was here late at night. It must have been around midnight."

"What were you doing here so late?" Mark couldn't tell if this was a threatening question or just routine. Evers had the perfect poker face for a detective. Mark couldn't help but worry someone had seen him and the twins in Cooley's office last night.

"Working, of course." Technically this wasn't a lie, Mark thought to himself. "There's a lot of work to catch up on for a new Senator."

Evers didn't look up as he made notes.

"Was you secretary here with you?"

"No, she wasn't." Although this was the truth, the question still made Mark uncomfortable.

There was no reaction from Evers as he continued to scribble.

"Did you hear anyone come in?"

"No."

"Then how did the assailant gain access to your office?"

"I really don't know?"

"Were you here the entire evening?"

Immediately Mark knew he had to tell the truth which, thankfully for Mark, provided an explanation for how the assailant entered Mark's office without Mark knowing. Mark just hoped Evers didn't ask where he was.

"No, I stepped out for an hour or so to handle some personal matters."

Again Evers showed no facial reaction to Mark's answer. "Hum, out an hour for personal matters," Evers muttered as he wrote the words. Fortunately for Mark, there was no follow-up.

"It makes sense then the perpetrator gained entry while you were away and was waiting for you. Do you think the perpetrator knew you were coming back?"

"Lt. Evers, I have no idea."

Evers now looked up from his notepad. "Now Senator Williams, have you been able to determine if anything from your office is missing? Does it appear the assailant took anything?"

Mark wondered how far he should go in telling Evers about the MI6 report. If he revealed the report and the fact it was from Senator Cooley, Mark would have to explain how he got it. Thinking quickly, Mark decided he could finesse the answer.

"Yes, I have determined I'm missing a report I was reading about possible foreign influence in some of our domestic affairs."

"Foreign influence?" Evers had stopped writing and was looking directly at Mark's face.

"Can I assume, Lt. Evers, you will be discreet with the information I share with you?"

"Senator Williams, I am only interested in solving a murder and an assault on two U.S. Senators. The information you have is only relevant if it helps me solve those two cases. Do we understand each other?"

"I understand, and yes I do. The document talked about a possible plot by France and Spain to build up support in the U.S. for a constitutional convention. The report was written by the British version of our CIA, MI6."

"I know what MI6 is," Evers responded tartly. "Were Senator Cooley or you mentioned in the report?"

"No we weren't."

More scribbling. "How did you obtain this report?"

"I obtained it from Senator Cooley." Mark was happy this was technically true.

"I assume before she died."

Mark had no choice but to lie. "Yes."

"OK, Senator Williams, I have enough for now. From what you've told me, it does appear Senator Cooley's murder and your assault may be related. This is helpful, very helpful. I'm sure we'll be talking again. I wish I could post a guard in your office, but I just don't have the manpower. I hope you understand."

"I understand, but thanks all the same."

"I'll show myself out."

As soon as Evers left, Denise hurried into Mark's office.

"Since I made that big boo-boo with the cup, I wanted to stay away from that policeman so I wouldn't cause any more trouble for you. Did he ask any hard questions? Did you tell him about our little visit to Senator Cooley's office last night?"

Always multiple questions for Denise, the last of which Mark thought was somewhat odd. "No, he doesn't know about our late night break-in to Senator Cooley's office. I still feel bad about that."

Denise moved to the back of Mark's chair and suddenly began massaging his shoulders.

"You're really tense. This will help." The work of her fingers on his shoulders felt totally relaxing to Mark. "And I need to look at that pump on your head and replace the band aid. But that can wait until later."

Denise swiftly moved in front of Mark's chair to face him. She untied her hair bun, letting her blond-brown hair flow to her shoulders. Then she unbuttoned her blouse and stood before him with only a bra covering her breasts. Next Denise moved toward Mark, perched herself on his legs, and pulled both his arms to the hooks of her bra against her back.

Mark was so surprised by Denise's unexpected movements that he had no time to react. The primal part of him immediately noticed how enticing Denise was. She always looked attractive in her professional clothing, but the Denise without that clothing was sensual, appealing, and available. Within seconds Mark became aroused.

"I wanted you the first time I saw you," Denise whispered in Mark's ear. "You need to have some fun. You deserve some fun, and I can give it to you."

Mark wanted to. His fingers were ready to unclasp Denise's bra when the logical side of his brain took command.

"Denise, I can't." Mark gently lifted her off is knees, placing her feet on the floor. "I'm flattered someone as young and attractive as you finds me appealing, but I'm devoted to my wife and boys and to the integrity of the Senate."

Denise wasn't ready to give up. "If you're worried that people will talk, they won't. These trysts go on all the time in the Senate."

Mark was already up and straightening his tie and smoothing his hair. "Again, Denise, you are a lovely woman. Any man would be lucky to have a relationship with you. But that man is not me. We'll keep our relationship professional.

Denise shared an apartment with Darlene on Connecticut Ave., a short subway ride from the Capitol. Darlene was already home when Denise arrived.

Darlene was in one of the two rockers in the living room sipping a glass of wine. "Did you score?"

"No, not yet. He's still hooked on fidelity."

"Too bad. He's a looker. Take me. I had to deal with Miss Queen Bee, Cooley. You know me. I don't swing that way. Now that she's gone, maybe I'll be lucky to get a stud replacement."

Denise now had a glass of wine and had sunk into the other rocker. "What do you mean? I read there are now 64 different types of sexual preferences. You just don't know which type you are."

Darlene took another sip of wine. "Oh, I know what type I am. The type that wants a real man, just like Mark Williams. Want me to take a run at him?"

"Don't you dare," smiled Denise. "He's all mine. And, by the way, tonight wasn't all for nothing. I have a backup plan."

"Good. And speaking of the late Senator Cooley, you know who I'd like to have a roll in the hay with? That ex-husband of hers. Oh my, what a hunk, even though he's in his 60s. Tall, dark, fit, and you know what they say about Black men. Yes, ma'am, I'd jump him in a heartbeat."

"I hope you get your chance. Or maybe I'll beat you to it."

Denise and Darlene clinked their glasses.

After glancing through the *Post*, Denise asked, "What's on the telly tonight?"

CHAPTER 13

Governor's Office, Phoenix Arizona, Tuesday, January 4, Early Morning

THERESA HAD JUST REACHED HER DESK IN THE GOVERNOR'S OFFICE when Emily, who had worked for her since Theresa entered public service, buzzed her.

"Governor, I know you probably haven't even sat down yet, but I have a call from someone you likely want to talk to. It's the Governor of California, Al Suarez. Should I say you'll just be a minute?"

Theresa plopped in her chair. The recent confrontation with Luis and now the news about the federal default made her want to just have a little quiet time. But it looked like quiet time would be rare when you're the Governor.

"Yes, tell him I'll be with him momentarily." Theresa needed at least a few seconds to compose herself.

"Governor Suarez, how nice of you to call." Theresa did her best to sound cheerful.

"Governor Vargas. Let me be one of the first to congratulate you on becoming Governor of the great state of Arizona. You know, if I didn't live in California, I'd choose Arizona. I absolutely love your state."

"I bet you tell that to all the Governors." Theresa meant it as a joke but she knew it was true.

Suarez let out a loud laugh - too loud - thought Theresa to

be genuine. Suarez was a throwback to politicians of the past, someone who loved shaking hands, slapping backs, kissing babies, and talking. That breed of politician had largely disappeared as campaigns increasing used social media, staged rallies, and controlled interviews. While Suarez's personality was often phony, at least he had a personality. As the first Hispanic Governor elected in California, his election was helped by the Hispanic majority in the state. Yet he wasn't a one-note governor. Having made a fortune in avocado farming, he understood California's big problems. High taxes and lavish spending had caused the state to lose over a fourth of its high profile tech and entertainment industries. A big bet on solar power had only resulted in energy shortages and high utility bills. Then there was California's chronic shortage of water for its population of almost 50 million.

"Theresa – I hope I can call you Theresa, and please call me Al – I just received news the federal government has defaulted. Have you heard this? It's not a surprise. With the mess in Washington, it was just a matter of time."

"Yes, I just learned about the federal default, Al." Theresa wondered where the conservation was headed.

"I'm glad you know, so we're on the same page. Here's the deal, and you may not know this since you've just taken the reins of office. The default presents a big problem for us at the state level. Traditionally the federal government has helped states with a variety of spending programs, like transportation, education, health care, food stamps, and so on."

"Yes, I know Al. I was a state senator for eight years."

"Of course you were, and I didn't mean to imply you aren't aware of these programs." Al immediately liked Theresa's spunk. Yet this also meant she wouldn't be a pushover, so he'd have to be at the top of his game. "With federal budgeting so inept in recent years, the only way states received funds for these programs was by the federal government borrowing the money. The revenue from the income tax the feds collect, while large, has been dropping with lax IRS enforcement. And most of that tax money now goes to paying federal bureaucrats and the military, and it's still not doing that very well."

"Hopefully the default will motivate Congress and the President to produce a real budget that raises sufficient revenue, pays the bills, and adequately services the national debt," Theresa interjected.

Al wanted to respond, 'don't count on it, sweetheart,' but that would be political suicide for what he needed from Theresa. He continued in a professional manner.

"The problem in a nutshell, Theresa, is California still pays almost half a trillion dollars to the federal government each year, and now we'll be lucky to get a dime back. With this default and little likelihood of things turning around in Washington, we're better off without the federal government."

Theresa's mind was rapid-fire fast. It had to be with all the unexpected decisions that would come up on active construction sites. She found that ability also helped her make quick assessments in the political world, and that was one reason why people admired her.

"Thanks for this heads-up, Al. I'll have my budget people look at it right away. I'm sure it will be helpful for us to share some possible solutions once we've had time to formulate them."

"Hold on Theresa. I already have a solution."

"Oh, you do? What is it?" Theresa was curious but also guarded.

Now Al was at the point in the conversation he was waiting for. He had to give Theresa his best sales pitch, as only a politician could.

"The solution is, we don't need the federal government. In fact, we don't want the federal government, because they're costing us money. Think of what I could do with half a trillion dollars every year. I think your gain would be about a hundred billion annually." In fact, Arizona's gain was exactly that – Al's people had already done the calculations.

"So, what do you propose? Seceding from the federal government? Theresa sharply interjected. "That was tried already and wasn't successful. It led to several hundred thousand deaths in a war lasting four years." Theresa had hoped she could get through the call with Suarez without getting testy, but that wasn't to be.

"No, certainly not. Bloodshed it not the answer. My solution has two simple steps. First, Arizona joins California and four other states in the WSF – Western States Federation. It's already formed and we're looking to get most of the states west of the Missouri River to join, including the Colorado, Texas, and your neighbor, New Mexico. States in the WSF will coordinate their fiscal policies, take advantage of economies of scale in spending, and – this is very important – the member states won't compete with each other in offering big incentives packages to lure new businesses. Don't I remember that last year your state dangled $200 million in incentives to entice Walboard to locate in Arizona rather than California? We won't do those kinds of things in the WSF. We'll cooperate instead of compete."

Theresa thought Al's pitch sounded well-rehearsed. With changes in a couple of numbers, he could make it to any governor.

"What's the second step?"

Al paused before answering. He knew this could be the closer line. When he uttered the words, he would have to sound sincere, strong, and convincing.

"The second step is for Arizona to join California and other current or prospective WSF states in calling for a new constitutional convention. We want Arizona to be a proud part of Concon. Concon is the only way our country will get back on its feet and achieve its true potential" - Al paused for effect – "for everyone."

"Wow, those are two big steps, Al. Your proposal is going to take considerable thought and discussion and include a variety of viewpoints. It's not something I – and Arizona – can take lightly. Our country will never be the same after Concon."

"Of course, of course, Theresa, you and Arizona take some time. Just remember, the clock is ticking. There's nothing gained from waiting. Indeed, there's potentially much to be lost. Please call me anytime to discuss this. And again, my hearty congratulations on your first day in office. I hope you'll always remember it."

"Thank you, Governor, I will. Your call will be memorable."

Suarez wasn't sure how to interpret Theresa's comment, which was exactly how Theresa intended it.

Theresa knew there certainly was a logic to Suarez's argument for WSF and Concon. Still, Suarez made WSF sound like an 'all for one and one for all' concept. Theresa didn't necessarily see it that way. A large deposit of natural gas had just been discovered in Arizona. Despite continued public cries from various groups for California to become totally fossil-fuel free, privately those same groups would love to take control of Arizona's gas to ease California's energy crunch. Also, California had long sought to take more water from the Colorado River where it formed the boundary between California and Arizona. Bottom line -Theresa saw a lot of bare-knuckled politics in Suarez's pitch.

In Sacramento, Governor Suarez was also assessing his conversation with Governor Vargas. He concluded she would need more convincing.

CHAPTER 14

Washington, DC, Tuesday, January 4, Mid Afternoon

CAROL AND TONY SLEPT UNTIL 2 PM. NEITHER OF THEM HAD EVER slept that late in the day. After showering and dressing, they had some kind of meal – they really didn't know what to call it given the time of day - at the Econolodge, then bought a *Post* and scanned the help-wanted section. They did see a big ad for the British Embassy.

"They certainly are hiring." Carol pointed to a long list of job openings in the ad. "Here's a bunch of tech jobs for you. They're more limited for me. Probably the best is this one for editing and fact checking reports and press releases." Carol had her finger on the job description as she looked at Tony.

"I say we take the metro and check out those jobs right now."

Carol and Tony were used to riding the New York subways when the visited 'the City,' as the locals called it. But the DC Metro had their New York counterparts beat. While New York subways were generally dirty, crowded, and frequently late, by comparison the DC Metro was punctual, lightly used, and clean. Still, Carol and Tony sat close together and watched everyone who boarded.

The Metro dropped them about ten blocks from the British Embassy on Massachusetts Ave. They had a little bit of a hike, but the couple enjoyed looking at the stately structures as they walked along the historic street. The Embassy was an imposing red brick building built in the 1930s to resemble an English manor house. It also was the Ambassador's residence. The grounds were completely gated with guards at the main entrance. The couple could see a statue of Winston Churchill in the side gardens.

A sign at the front gate directed them to go to the next building, which – according the Doug – the British also owned. With an exterior of darker red brick, the structure looked much more common, almost like an office building. If they were able to get jobs, the couple hoped they would work in the mansion.

Carol and Tony followed arrows up a sidewalk to a side entrance. Even though it was just past 9, there was already a short line. Fortunately, it only took about 15 minutes for them to reach a desk, where each was given a form to complete. They moved into a large open room with the other applicants and sat in folding chairs behind a long metal table.

The form asked for the usual information, including age, gender, email, phone number, citizenship, education, and special skills. Carol and Tony listed their degrees - Tony's in computer science and logistics, and Carol's in British history. When they returned the forms to the secretary, they were expecting to hear a 'we'll contact you' response.

The secretary – a middle-aged woman with an English accent - perused their forms. "Interesting. You two are married?"

"Yes we are, a little over a year," Carol replied proudly.

"I want you to take these forms to Mr. Headly in the main Embassy next door. I'll buzz the guards to be expecting you. They'll direct you to Mr. Headly's office and he'll take it from there."

Carol and Tony were surprised but pleased. Tony answered for the couple. "Thank you very much. Mr. Headly, right? We'll look forward to meeting him." Tony then grabbed the secretary's hand and gave it a couple of quick shakes. She responded with a slight smile, handed him the forms, and then said, "On with you now."

"I can't believe this." Tony was on cloud 9. Maybe we'll get jobs today."

Reversing their usual attitudes, Carol was now the calm and realistic one. "Remember what my Mom always says. 'Expect the worst but hope for the best.' We want to appear interested and eager, but not over-excited. If they think we're desperate, they might low-ball our salaries."

"Now look who's expecting the best," smiled Tony.

The couple retraced their steps to the front gate of the main Embassy, showed the guard their forms, and were let in and directed to the front door, where someone else would take over. As Tony passed the Churchill statue, he gave the World War II hero a salute. Carol grinned and playfully shook her head, even though she felt goosebumps walking through the garden.

A young man at the door greeted them and asked the couple to follow him down a long hallway. Both Carol and Tony had to keep their mouths from gasping. The hallway walls were a deep walnut wood. Carefully spaced were portraits mainly of males. Carol guessed they were former ambassadors. The overhead lights were small, delicate chandeliers which provided a subdued effect not clashing with the tiny portrait lights over each painting.

At the fifth door on the right, their guide stopped, knocked, and then upon hearing 'enter,' opened the door and directed Carol and Tony to go in. As they passed the guide, he whispered 'good luck.'

Immediately a bald, slightly overweight man with a modest mustache and dressed in a dapper three-piece blue suit walked around his desk and extended his hand. "Good morning, I'm Albert Headly, Deputy Head of Human Resources at the British Embassy. Mr. and Mrs. Shipman, please, each of you take a seat."

Carol and Tony both thanked Headly as he moved back to his desk chair. They each sat in a comfortable dark wood chair with red cushioning facing Headly's desk.

"Both of you have impressive degrees from Cornell, one of America's best so-called 'Ivy League' universities. I have often found what's more important is the quality of the school rather than the specific major. But in your cases, you attended a school we admire and specialized in majors we can use. But, of course, we will need to verify your credentials before offering you jobs."

Outside of Headly's view, Carol took Tony's hand and gave it a quick squeeze.

"You list your address as a local Econolodge. Is that some kind of hotel?"

Tony cleared his throat. "Yes, it is, Mr. Headly. See, we're new to the area, and until we get jobs, the Econolodge is very affordable."

Carol wasn't happy Tony revealed they were essentially poor, and Tony regretted saying it as soon as the words left his mouth. But Headly didn't appear to be phased.

"Well, let me welcome you to your country's capital. I'm from the Midlands in England, but I've worked all around the world. Your capital has fabulous museums, wonderful restaurants, and reasonable rents – especially compared to many world capitals. Also, I must admit I've become a fan of your game of baseball, which, of course, originated from our game of cricket."

"Both Carol and I are Met's fans."

"Ah, yes, the Mets. Big rivals of our local Nats. I'd say the Nats have had the better of the Mets in recent years, including – what do you call it – ah, yes, the champs of the World Series. Which is actually a detour to my next question. Why did you leave New York and come to Washington? Was it for a better baseball team?" Headly's grin was hidden by his mustache.

Carol and Tony didn't know how much to say, and it was too bad they couldn't talk about the question first before answering. If Headly suspected they were essentially fugitives from New York, Carol wondered if that would count against them. Tony wondered if New York had sent their names to other states. Maybe their names were traced from the abandoned Forrester in Pennsylvania.

Carol decided to be honest. "Mr. Headly, we're two young people just starting out in life. Someday we want to have a family. Jobs and the economy in New York just aren't good. We decided there were better opportunities here in Washington." Carol decided to omit the fact their real destination was Raleigh.

Headly leaned back in his chair and looked approvingly at the couple. "I admire initiative, and I understand what you're saying about New York. We have been monitoring the changes in the economies of the various U.S. states for many years. New York has certainly been hit with some hard times."

Carol and Tony nodded, but were silent.

"I'm going to recommend both of you be hired. As you saw, we are expanding our functions here. The breakup of the European Union has caused His Majesty's government to reassess its geopolitical positions and relationships. One relationship we definitely plan to expand is with the United States."

Almost in unison, Carol and Tony both said 'thank you.' Then Tony added, "What will we be doing?"

"For you, Tony, your computer skills, especially in logistics and data management, are highly valued. I imagine we'll put you in a mid-level position with a small staff."

Next, Headly looked at Carol. "I've always thought historians were undervalued. Perspective is vital in diplomacy, and historians by nature have perspective. Even more, your Ph.D. in British history means you know us and how we think. Most people don't." Following the last comment, Headly let out a little chuckle. "Plus, you speak French. As you may or may not know, the French are restructuring their foreign policy in light of the EU's demise. There are significant French interests in North America, so knowing the French language is a valuable asset. In addition, historians tend to be good writers. With all of your skills, Carol, I envision you helping us write and edit reports and press releases as well as doing some research.

Carol and Tony were ecstatic. Inwardly they were giving each other high-fives.

Headly rose, suggesting the interview was over. Carol and Tony also stood.

"As I said, we'll need to validate your credentials and check on a few other things with your government. But unless you're secret ax-murderers," - Headly feinted fright by holding up his hands in a defensive posture – "then I think you should be hearing from us in a couple of days. We'll call you at one of the cell numbers you provided. Congratulations. We look forward to having you work for

His Majesty's government. And by the way, the salary for each of you will be 1000 US dollars a week."

Carol and Tony again thanked Headly, each of them shook his hand (the couple didn't think hugs were appropriate with a proper Englishman), and then left the Embassy. All the way Carol hummed 'God Save the King.'

Once outside and several buildings away from the Embassy, they embraced and Tony let out a big 'yahoo.' "Boy, with each us making $1000 a week, we'll gross around $100,000 a year. We'll be able to accumulate a nice little nest egg for our ultimate move to Raleigh."

"First thing we should do is look for a better place to live," offered Carol.

"Definitely," agreed Tony. "Then we should celebrate."

With a naughty look on her face, Carol added, "I know how."

CHAPTER 15

Governor's Residence, Phoenix Arizona, Wednesday, January 5, Mid Morning

ARIZONA IS ONE OF THE FEW STATES WITHOUT AN OFFICIAL Governor's Mansion. Typically states have ornate, historic homes dedicated to housing the Governor and his or her family. Not so for Arizona. There is an old, slightly dilapidated log cabin that once served as the Governor's residence, but it is now used as a tourist attraction.

Realizing Governors need special security, the Arizona legislature allocates monies to rent a home for the Governor. The home is jointly chosen by the Governor and her security staff.

Theresa picked a two-story craftsman structure in an historic neighborhood a few blocks from the Governor's office. The home had only 2000 square feet, but this was enough for Theresa, her daughter Flores, two personal assistants, and the three-person security staff. The security staff took one room downstairs as a command post, with a rotation for one of the team to stay overnight. The personal assistants, who did cooking, cleaning, and other chores for the Governor, took another room but did not sleep on site. This left the kitchen, dining room, and an office for Theresa on the first floor. The four upstairs rooms were Theresa and Flores' private quarters. Theresa and Flores had moved into the bungalow two weeks before the inauguration.

Theresa could not be prouder of Flores. A high school junior, Flores was unlike most of her peers. She found technology useful, but was not hooked to social media. Nor did she allow social media to dictate her likes, dislikes, and self-esteem. Flores wanted to me an engineer like her mother, and had the grades to prove it. Although engaging and attractive – combining her mother's copper coloring and almond eyes with her father's Nordic features – Flores didn't yet date. Her focus was on school, family, and – somewhat secretly – her mother's political career. Theresa often wondered what she did to deserve such a great kid.

"So, Mom, you have your first press conference today. Are you excited and maybe a little scared?" While talking, Flores eagerly eyed her bowl of oatmeal, raisins, orange juice, and hot cocoa being prepared by the cook, Lisa.

"I think I'm prepared, and I'm anxious to have the forum to present my agenda for this session of the legislature." Most teens' eyes would glaze over upon hearing 'agenda' and 'legislature', but not Flores. She hung on every one of her Mother's words. "Scared – no, I don't think so, although that may change when I see all the reporters and cameras in front of me."

Theresa picked her clothing for this important day to reflect Arizona's official colors. She wore a smart-looking, matching red skirt and jacket suit with blue trim and a wide bright yellow belt. The red and blue were taken from the U.S. flag and represented Arizona's pride in being the 48th U.S. state. Red and yellow were colors of Spain's national flag and honored the state's original explorers from that European country. Theresa also wore a prominent copper-colored star-shaped necklace. The color paid tribute to Arizona being the largest copper producer in the country.

Theresa's mother, Maria, always provided her children with a substantial and filling breakfast, and Theresa continued that tradition even after she started living on her own. She regularly ate two scrambled eggs, two link sausages, one lightly buttered piece of whole wheat toast, orange juice, and coffee. The only difference now was Lisa prepared it for her.

"Mom, you look absolutely glamorous. You're going to wow everyone in that outfit as well as with your brains. What kind of questions do you think you'll get?"

Theresa considered the question while she chewed her first piece of egg and finished a sip of juice. "They could be on anything. There'll be lots on the budget I'll submit to the legislature. We're just beginning to put it together, so I'll only be able to answer in generalities, which will make some reporters mad. The environment and energy are chronic issues in our state, so I'm sure I'll have some questions about those issues."

Theresa paused for more food, and Flores took advantage of the opening. "What about Concon, the call for a constitutional convention for the country. That guy Fuentes is running ads everywhere supporting it. He's even demanding you support it."

Theresa was surprised and a little concerned.

"You've heard about Concon?"

"Oh sure, who hasn't? The Fuentes ads are pretty slick and fun to watch."

Theresa stopped eating and put down her fork. "Flores, do you support Concon?" Theresa was afraid of what Flores would say. Polls showed support for Concon was high among Hispanic youth, such as Luis and Armando. Theresa was afraid Flores may had fallen prey to the charms of Fuentes' ads.

Not sensing the gravity of the question, Flores cheerfully answered it like any other. "For sure I'm opposed to Concon. I know our country has problems, but we'll eventually fix them. We always have. Look at the discrimination against Gays, Blacks, and even Hispanics. I know everyone's not on board, but the vast majority of people just consider people to be people. You're Hispanic and not a citizen; yet you're Governor. The President is gay. The CEO of Facebook is Black. Neighborhoods are no longer red-lined, and whether someone gets a loan doesn't depend on skin color. The Concon people just want to just use a convention to break up our country. That's not right. Mom, I want you to stop it."

Theresa had to fight back tears. For the first of many times today, she would ask herself, how did she get such a daughter?

The press conference was held shortly after lunch in the large general-purpose room down the hall from Theresa's office in the Capitol. The room was packed with around 150 people sitting and standing. Cameras from all the major networks and local channels were trained on the podium.

Theresa was introduced by her press secretary with a simple, "Ladies, and Gentlemen, Governor Vargas."

Theresa strode confidently to the podium, placed a few notes on the slanted top, and then began. "Members of the press, thank you for coming to my first press conference. I hope to make this a regular event to further my goal of staying in touch with our great citizens. I do have a few ground rules. First, questioners get only one follow-up question. Two, I won't necessarily call on the person who shouts the loudest." There were some manufactured moans at this. "And three, I expect you to spell my name correctly. It's v-a-r-g –A- s, not v-a-r-g-U-s. Some of you got it wrong during the campaign." There were a few chuckles. "Now, I'll take the first question. Yes, John."

"John Richter of the *Arizona Republic*." The oldest newspaper in the state, the reporter for the *Republic* typically got the first question. "Governor, you were a strong advocate of K-12 education while a state senator. I assume you will continue that passion as Governor. How do you intend to fund the initiatives you've talked about, like higher teacher pay, smaller class sizes, and the controversial idea of boarding room schools for certain students?"

"Excellent questions." When she entered politics, Theresa was told by a long-time politician to always complement the questioner, whether she liked the question or not. "I'll only give you a brief outline here. The details will be in my forthcoming budget. I am passionate about K, really pre-K, to 12 education. Research has clearly shown that higher pay attracts better teachers, and when you combine better teachers with smaller class sizes, you see great performance by students. And, by the way, boarding room schools are not controversial. They are ideal for students living in challenging backgrounds. And they'll only be used with the consent of the parent or guardian.

"And how will you pay for these?" Richter knew politicians liked to avoid the payment issue.

"John, I was just about to address that. I will consider a combination of three approaches. First are higher business taxes, particularly an increase in the state corporate income tax. I'll talk to business leaders and explain how better educated citizens help them hire better trained workers who are more productive, and who earn more and then spend more. Second, I'll look for savings in higher education. We need to have more college students graduate on time, in four years. If we can increase the percentage of students graduating in four years from today's 33% to eventually 50%, the state saves $300 million annually. Last, I'm having my staff thoroughly examine the budgets of every state agency with the goal of finding savings, hopefully in the hundreds of millions of dollars. I'll put these savings, along with those from higher education spending, into pre-K to 12 education."

Theresa surveyed the room as hands went up and then pointed at a reporter from KPNX, the Phoenix NBC affiliate. "Yes, Miss Starling."

"Thank you, Governor, and let me offer my congratulations on your election." 'Suck-up' mumbled one reporter under his breath. "In the state senate you were an opponent of the call for a national constitutional convention, also known as Concon. Polls show Arizonians evenly split on this issue. There are now new ads running calling on you to change your mind and support Concon. Will you?"

Theresa was emphatic. "No." There were murmurs in the room because politicians were rarely so blunt. "I continue to oppose Concon, and I see no reason to expect I will change my mind. In fact, just this morning I discussed Concon with my 17-year old daughter." A veteran reporter turned to his colleague and quietly whispered, 'Here we go again. Just like Jimmy Carter seeking advice about nuclear weapons from his teenage daughter Amy.' Both snickered. "She, like me, recognizes the country has many problems. Yet our U.S. Constitution has served us well for almost 250 years, and I think it will continue to do so. I believe there is no problem we ...."

In another part of Phoenix the TV was abruptly clicked off. "I've seen enough. She's not going to change her stand on Concon. We have to change it for her. Tell the unit to put the operation in motion."

CHAPTER 16

The Capitol, Washington, DC, Wednesday, January 5, Mid Afternoon

THE U.S. CONSTITUTION ALLOWS A CONSTITUTIONAL CONVENTION to be called with the approval of at least two-thirds of the state legislatures. Left unsaid in the Constitution is what 'approval' by a state legislature really means. Most people would think approval means a majority of the members of a legislature voted for a Constitutional Convention. But what 'most people would think' and what 'politicians actually do' can be two entirely different things.

Mark stood in the well of the Senate chambers. He was glad to have time away from the office, and especially away from Denise. Since the 'encounter,' their interactions had been awkward, with both doing the best they could to avoid the other.

The Senate leadership, which, at least for today, was composed of the States' Rights, Alt-Right, Tea, and Green parties – or 'Straw-Teg' for short - had scheduled a floor debate on legislation authorizing new rules for states to follow in considering a call for a Constitutional Convention. The House had already passed its version, which lowered the threshold for a state's approval to 40% of its legislators voting yes. The Senate was now considering the same. With the reduced approval margin, Concon would easily become a reality.

Mark mingled with several other Senators, introducing himself and sharing basic information such as party affiliation, family life, and career before politics. The majority of Senators were still lawyers. While smart, Mark saw a big problem with lawyers in politics. They tended to think everything could be solved with a law, ignoring the likelihood – proven many times – that people and companies will usually find ways around laws. Mark thought a little more perspective and understanding of human behavior would be useful in the Senate, and he believed his work in business had provided that.

"Hey Mark, welcome to the 'Show.' This is where it all happens." Joe Ferguson loved baseball and the *Atlanta Braves* and adopted the word players used to describe the major leagues.

"It sure is good to see a friendly face." Mark and Joe pumped each other's hand. "The other senators aren't exactly welcoming. I thought the Senate was collegial, even among those with different views."

"Unfortunately, Mark, like the rest of the country, the Senate has changed a lot in the last few decades. There was a time when party enemies could still be good friends. Jesse Helms and Ted Kennedy were two senators on the opposite ends of the political spectrum, yet in private they were friendly and gracious with each other. Helms – who many publicly called a racist – would probably have been voted the most generous and polite senator by his colleagues."

"It's not that way now?" Mark surmised.

"Oh, no." Ferguson guided the pair to a vacant section of the room to be out of earshot. "It's all vicious now. Whatever it takes to win will be done. Your opponent is not someone to debate over the merits of positions, but is a person to be despised, hated, and destroyed. And it's not just for show. Insults and accusations used to be hurled by opponents in public, but in private they made jokes about their performances over drinks. Now the venom is for real. Senators badmouth their opponents both here and at home. Recently I heard one senator label another promoting an opposing view as evil and unfit to live. And she meant it."

"I had no idea it was this bad."

"That's because you were widely popular in South Carolina, so your opponents didn't spend a lot of time and money trashing you.

But if they thought they could have destroyed you and won, they would have tried."

Mark and Ferguson were interrupted by the sound of a gavel. The Senate was being called into order by the Vice President, Shandra Lee, who also had the title of President of the Senate. Vice Presidents usually didn't exercise their constitutional role to preside over the Senate unless the issue being considered was very important. Clearly Vice President Lee, a member of the States' Rights Party, believed the floor debate and possible vote on Concon rules to be worth her time.

"The Senate will come to order," commanded Lee. "The order of business is debate over Senate Bill 425, which has the Senate authorizing new rules for states to follow in authorizing a Constitutional Convention. Senator Avent, you have the floor."

Mavis Avent, the former Black mayor of Murfreesboro, Tennessee, was the leader of the Straw-Teg coalition in the Senate and hence Majority Leader. As long as the coalition remained intact, Avent controlled the agenda of the Senate. One of the issues uniting Straw-Teg was their support of Concon. The States' Rights, Alt-Right, Tea, and Green parties were all inherently suspicious of the federal government. The first three were leery on principle, while the Greens thought the federal government was too cozy with polluters. The parties would cheer a dismantling of the federal government and an elevation of individual state control.

Avent approached her podium. "Madam President, the Senate will now devote five and a half hours of debate to Senate Bill 425. Senators are limited to three minutes, with the ability to yield unused time to designated colleagues. At the halfway point in time, there will be a 30-minute break, but – I emphasize – no more than that. Senators who miss their turn to speak will not be given another." Even those opposed to Avent's politics liked the efficient meetings she ran.

For the rest of the afternoon and into the evening Mark listened to the debate pro and con over Bill 425. Supporters didn't hide the fact they wanted a constitutional convention so they could weaken the federal government. They wanted a constitution more along the lines of the original Articles of Confederation, which kept most of the power – including the power of the purse – in the hands of the states.

Opponents wanted the opposite – a limited, yet strong, federal government. They emphasized the importance of a strong federal government for national defense, for promoting interstate commerce and a growing economy, and for linking the states through an extensive interstate transportation system of highways, airports, and the new hyperloop, through which travel could approach 700 miles per hour. Opponents pointed to the existing 10th amendment the Constitution, which left powers not enumerated to the federal government to the states, to show they were also attentive to states' rights.

Mark yielded his time to Joe Ferguson, preferring to listen attentively to the opposing arguments. Yet nothing that was said changed his mind. His views on Concon were clearly stated during his senate campaign. He agreed with opponents that Concon backers wanted to use the convention to dismantle the federal government and effectively end the United States of America.

The gavel was pounded again, and Vice President Lee again called on Majority Leader Avent. "Madam President, with the Senate's debate over Bill 425 complete, I have consulted the Minority Leader and he has agreed with me to schedule a vote one week from today at 10 am."

Lee scanned the chambers. "Hearing no objection, the vote on Senate Bill 435 will be held on January 17 at 10 am. The Senate is adjourned."

Mark left his desk to begin the walk to the Senate subway, which would take him back to the Dirksen Building and his office. He received some glances and even a couple polite nods, but Mark was somewhat surprised no colleague approached him to lobby for a vote either for or against the bill. Actually, Mark was relieved. He didn't really enjoy debating, or any kind of confrontation for that matter.

Maybe everyone knew is position was firm, so there was no use wasting time trying to change his vote.

Just as he was about ten feet away from the subway, a thin male maybe late 20s in age and dressed in a standard business-grey suit approached. Mark didn't recognize him.

"Hey, Senator Williams, way to go." The smile looked genuine and the tone was friendly. "I saw on today's Hotspot website that you've already gotten some. That-a-way. When the wife leaves, the play begins." After delivering those comments, the stranger sprinted away down the walkway.

Mark's brain reeled. What did the stranger mean? What had Mark already 'gotten'? Then it dawned on him. Was it a reference to Denise's romantic advance the other night, just after Cheryl had left for South Carolina? If so, how did the stranger know? But more important, what did it mean for Mark, his career, and his vote on Bill 425?

CHAPTER 17

Phoenix, Arizona, Thursday, January 6, Early Morning

It happened suddenly and without warning. It was just before dawn, at about 5:30 am. Maria had always been an early riser. Eugenio had to be at construction sites as soon as it was light enough to work. Also, Maria thought it was essential to prepare complete and nutritious breakfasts for her three children, and this took time. Even though Eugenio had passed and her children were on her own, Maria's habits still hadn't changed. She was always up early making eggs, sausage, toast, and coffee for herself.

Although her eyes had deteriorated and she needed to wear glasses, Maria's hearing was still superb. So when they walked onto her porch and approached the kitchen door, Maria heard them.

They were too fast. In seconds the kitchen door was kicked open. Three individuals wearing black masks and black jackets and pants stormed in to Maria's kitchen, grabbed her, and put a hood over her head while tying her hands together. Before Maria could scream, part of the hood was forced into her mouth. "Eso debería mantenerte callado," (That should keep you quiet) said one.

Two of the abductors carried Maria to a waiting black SUV while the third looked for anyone watching them. With precise efficiency, Maria was placed in between two kidnappers in the back seat. The third abductor slid in to the front seat next to the driver.

"Ir, ir" (go, go), said the assailant in the front passenger seat, who apparently was the leader.

Maria was shaking with fear and began to cry.

"Calme señora, no le haremos daño," (Be calm lady, we won't hurt you), whispered the abductor to her right.

Maria collected herself and focused on what she had taught Theresa.

The SUV headed south in the light morning traffic, the driver always watching to stay under the speed limit. Maria put her head back on the seat pretending to sleep. Only she wasn't.

The SUV travelled for about three and a half hours – as best Maria could determine – occasionally turning and sometimes making full stops at what likely were stoplights. Then, about 30 minutes later, Maria wondered if they were at the Mexican border. She thought she heard someone say, 'we've been expecting you; go on through.' Finally, the vehicle came to a complete stop with the engine cut off after roughly four and a half hours of travel – again with Maria guessing.

"Despierta mamá, este es tu nuevo hogar," (Wake up momma, this is your new home) said Maria's kidnapper on her left with a chuckle.

Maria was again carried by her two handlers around the SUV to the front door of a house. The door was opened, and – now walking – Maria was escorted in. Her hands were untied and the hood was removed. It took a couple minutes for her eyes to adjust to the light. When they did, she couldn't believe what she saw. Standing in front of Maria was Luis.

CHAPTER 18

Nogales, Mexico, Thursday, January 6, Late Morning

BOTH RELIEF AND ANGER GRIPPED MARIA. SHE RAN TO LUIS WHO let her embrace him in a tight squeeze.

Purposefully speaking English in hopes her abductors wouldn't understand, Maria spoke to Luiz, with fear lacing each word. "Luis, why did these men take me? Where am I, and why are you here?"

Saddened to see his mother treated like a criminal, Luis struggled to control his emotions.

"Momma, are you OK?" Luis looked at her wrists and saw red streaks from the ropes.

"¿Quién le hizo esto a mi mamá? El lo pagará" (Who did this to my momma? He'll pay for it), Luis shouted.

One of the guards shrugged.

"Momma, I'm so, so sorry, but it had to be done. Theresa wouldn't accept reasoning. We have to get her attention so she'll do the right thing."

"Luis, what do you mean, right thing?"

"Luis means supporting Concon, Mrs. Vargas." The words were spoken by Robert Fuentes, who had emerged from the next room. And, Mrs. Vargas, you can continue speaking English. Many of my employees don't speak it well, but I have perfect command of the English language."

Maria now recognized Fuentes. "You're the man on TV running

the commercials that say bad things about my daughter. Luis, why is this man here?"

Luis was quiet. Clearly Fuentes was in charge.

Fuentes approached Maria. Despite his name, Fuentes had Anglo characteristics. Tall, thin everywhere but in his gut, full grey hair, and dark skin that was not natural but came from constant tanning. He was wearing an expertly tailored beige suit with an open collared powder blue shirt. His shoes looked to be made of the skin of some kind of lizard. If someone looked quickly, Fuentes could easily be mistaken for an older and paunchy George Hamilton in his prime.

Fuentes extended his hand, but Maria refused. She boldly stated, "I want to go home."

Fuentes ignored her snub. "Mrs. Vargas, I'm Ricardo Fuentes. I apologize for all the dramatics. You will be going home in due time, but first we need something from your daughter, the Governor. We tried conventional methods – talking and explaining, advertising, and – I understand – even her siblings tried to convince her of the logic of our cause."

Maria shot a punishing look at Luis. Luis averted her eyes by looking down.

"Mrs. Vargas, let's sit." Fuentes motioned to a couch along the back wall of the room. "Are you thirsty or hungry? I can have my staff prepare you a small meal." Maria sat on the conch next to Luis, while Fuentes took an upholstered chair to the side of the couch.

Maria wanted to refuse, but she was very thirsty. Always polite, she asked, "May I have some coffee?"

"Of course." Fuentes snapped his fingers. "Miguel, coffee, quick." Miguel, who - from his tight sweater, clinging pants, and bulging muscles – looked like a bodybuilder, had been hovering discreetly across the room but watching intently. He could be Fuentes' bodyguard, personal goffer, or both.

"Now, Mrs. Vargas, while we're waiting for the coffee, let me explain my problem. Concon is the very popular national movement to create new constitutional convention to rid ourselves of the horrible United States national government. It is very close to becoming a reality. We only need a handful of states to add their approval, and Arizona is one of them. Yet your daughter has opposed us, first as a state senator and now as Governor. She just doesn't understand that Concon will be good for all of us."

The coffee arrived with silver cups and a large silver pot, all on a silver tray. Miguel sat it on the table in front of the couch and began pouring. Maria and Fuentes accepted cups, but Luis declined.

"Thank you, Miguel. That is all for now. Fuentes waited until Miguel left the room before continuing. "Your daughter has many followers, and even more now that she is Governor. If she said she supports Concon, I'm sure it would be approved in Arizona."

The coffee revived Maria and brought back her confidence. "I don't follow these things. Politics is confusing. I wouldn't know how to change my daughter's mind on this – how do you say – Concon."

Fuentes uttered a dismissive laugh. "No, Mrs. Vargas, we don't want you to debate your daughter. We just want you to tell her that when she publicly endorses Concon, you will be released. It's as easy as that. We'll set up a phone call, you'll talk, and then in a couple of days you'll be back in your lovely home."

Maria looked at Luis. He gently nodded his head.

"If I just tell my daughter to support Con, eh, Con, con, you'll let me go?"

"That's right, Mrs. Vargas, after we hear her support Concon publicly."

"OK, I'll talk to my daughter. But let me tell you, she can be hard to convince."

Fuentes smiled. "Oh, I think you can be very convincing Mrs. Vargas – very convincing."

After thinking, Maria had a question for Fuentes.

"Mr. Fuentes, if you don't mind, let me ask you one thing."

"Of course, Mrs. Vargas, anything."

"Aren't there many Concon supporters who want to see a new Mexican Empire created by putting the western U.S. states together with Mexico?"

A sly grin emerged on Fuentes' face. "Mrs. Vargas, what a

deceptive person you are. You do know more about Concon than you let on."

Although Maria despised Fuentes, she couldn't help appreciate the complement.

CHAPTER 19

The British Embassy, Washington, DC, Thursday, January 6, Late Morning

Carol and Tony found a one bedroom apartment to sublet on 34th St., only five blocks from the British Embassy. The lease was for four months, which coincided perfectly with the couple's plans to earn enough to purchase a used car for the trip to Raleigh. With employment contracts secured, they could now also upgrade their depleted wardrobes, since most of their clothes had been left behind in the Forrester abandoned in Pennsylvania. Carol noticed the staff at the Embassy dressed a couple of notches above what she was used to. Jeans and a casual shirt for Tony and blouse for Carol were out. After snuffing out an initial rebellion from him, Carol actually had fun picking out business slacks, long-sleeved button-down shirts, and even a few ties for Tony. For herself, she now had more skirts than ever in her life.

Carol's workspace was in the historic mansion. She found it exciting that the Ambassador's residence was upstairs, which was also where dignitaries, such as the Prime Minister, stayed on state visits. Carol shared a modestly sized room in the rear of the first floor with one other female and two males. They formed the 'writing and review' group. Their job was to edit already written reports and press releases, as well as to sometimes write those materials from scratch. Which task the unit performed depended on many things, including sensitivity of the document, the workloads of other units, and the expertise needed to compose the document. The U.S. British Embassy worked closely with its Canadian counterpart. Carol's fluency in French combined with her writing ability meant she could often be used to develop materials for the French-Canadian audience.

Tony was housed in the newly acquired building next to the mansion. The furnishing of the workspaces was just beginning. Tony was excited to see brand new top-of-the line computer equipment being delivered. He noticed most of the workspaces had multiple screens, something he was surprised to see in a government – albeit British – operation.

Tony was hanging out with a couple other newbies watching the equipment being unboxed when his cell phone buzzed.

"Hi, sweetie," announced Carol. "I thought I'd just check in and see how things are going."

"Great. I'm really excited about this job. Everything's going to be brand new and the latest available. These Brits have spared no expense. I should be hooked up and ready to go this afternoon. The head of this section – a guy named, get-this, Nigel Hamilton – will sit with each of us for a mini orientation. I think one of my jobs will be to monitor domestic websites for news content. Maybe something I stumble across will ultimately be sent to you."

"That would be amazing. The people over here are very nice. One – Natalie – is English and she's sort of the boss. The other two are guys and American. One of them has been here five years and loves it."

"Maybe we can get together for lunch in about an hour," hoped Tony. "It's actually sunny out. I know because there's one of those gigantic floor to ceiling windows in our office. It would be neat to eat outside in the garden, if only for a little bit."

"I agree. Let me see what's going on around noon and I'll text you. Love-ya."

"I love you too."

Although they considered their jobs temporary – something they didn't tell their supervisors – Carol and Tony actually enjoyed their work. Tony's main task was to monitor new sites – mainly of newspapers – across the southern half of the U.S., from Florida up to Virginia on the east coast and then across to California on the west coast. He had close to 75 sites to peruse daily. He also checked major national sites, such as *USA Today*, the *New York Times*, the *Washington Post*, and the *LA Times*, for national content pertaining to that region. When his manager, Nigel, became aware Tony had expertise in cyber security, he began involving Tony in some of the Embassy's security operations.

Most of Carol's time was spent checking for grammar, punctuation, and readability of the scores of press releases and reports the Embassy produced each week. The majority were done to create attention and praise for the UK among the American audience. The higher-ups in the Embassy kept track of how many of the releases were picked up by the American media. Much to Carol's pleasure, a number of the ones she edited found their way in to newspapers and evening TV broadcasts. Natalie praised Carol' work.

After returning from her lunch with Tony, Carol found Natalie waiting for her.

"Carol, I think I have something that will use your French. Take a look at this article from yesterday's *Le Monde*." *Le Monde* (The World) was considered the daily French newspaper of record, similar to *The New York Times* in the U.S. The French government often planted stories in *Le Monde* to gauge reactions to policies being considered.

Carol was excited to do something other than editing. Natalie walked across the room and left Carol alone. The article was about the Concon movement in the U.S. Carol hadn't followed Concon, but the article described it as similar to the cries for independence in the American colonies prior to the Revolutionary War. Immediately Carol could see why, even after 250 years, this could rub the British the wrong way.

Natalie walked back to Carol's desk after Carol finished the article.

"Pretty interesting, right? I don't speak or read French, but I've seen a translation." Natalie pulled up a spare chair to Carol's desk.

"I've been aware of Concon but I haven't followed it closely," Carol began. "I know this is ancient history, but I guess the comparison of the Concon backers to the American patriots of the 1700s and the heaping of praise on them is a little over the top. What would you like me to do?"

"I'd like you to write a press release describing the French analysis of Concon."

"And I'm guessing you want me to downplay or maybe even omit any references to the Revolution? Some people might interpret it as the French trying to interfere in U.S. politics."

"No, on the contrary. The bosses upstairs want you to include up front and center in the release those references and comparisons to the Revolutionary War and to throwing off oppressors. In fact, they want you to make them the focus of the press release."

CHAPTER 20

Phoenix, Arizona, Thursday, January 6, Late Morning

Theresa and Nick Phillips had been in a relationship for over a decade. Nick was a successful local architect who had met Theresa on a construction site where she was the lead engineer and he was the top architect. Nick was divorced with a son a year older than Flores. Nick's light Anglo-Saxon complexion perfectly complemented Theresa's copper toned skin. They made a striking couple on the power circuit of dinner parties and charity fund-raising dinners. Nick was also the yin to Theresa's yang. He was creative, spontaneous, and out-going to Theresa's straight line, controlled, and reserved personality. Theresa often thought Nick should have been the politician instead of her.

Numerous times they had discussed marriage. While they were committed to each other and wanted to spend the rest of their lives together, they worried about the possible impact of marriage on their children, who were now in those crucial adolescent years. Each of their children accepted – and actually embraced – the current status of the relationship between their parents. Theresa and Nick didn't want to do anything to upset that. Marriage could come later when their children were adults.

While an engineer and then as a state senator, Theresa regularly stayed at Nick's downtown condo. On those evenings Flores happily overnighted with her grandmother. Flores viewed it as a time for the two 'girls' to have fun. Thus far as Governor, Theresa had spent every night in the bungalow mansion.

Tonight would be the first time she wouldn't sleep at the bungalow as Governor. Tonight she would stay with Nick. Both were eagerly looking forward to the evening, as was Flores. Theresa's security detail first surveilled Nick's building and neighborhood. They were satisfied both passed the test for the safekeeping of the Governor. One of the officers would be on duty in the hallway outside Nick's entrance, while two more would patrol the outside of the building.

"I should be at your place around 7 unless some crisis occurs. It already seems like there's some fire to put out around every corner," lamented Theresa on her private cell phone to Nick.

"No worries." Nick had picked up some of the language of his largely millennial staff. "I still can't believe I'll be bedding the Governor of the State of Arizona."

"Be careful of your language, you rogue," teased Theresa. "I could have you arrested for threatening the Governor. But please promise you'll make good on the threat."

Nick laughed. "You wish. Besides me, I'll have a nice Pinot ready along with your favorite sushi and salad. I'll keep dessert a surprise."

"O-oo, I fell tingly all over. See you at 7."

It was 10 am and Theresa knew her mother had been up for several hours. She called Maria to reconfirm that Flores would be spending the night.

"Hum, that's odd," Theresa said to herself. She had let the phone ring seven times with no answer.

Theresa finished dressing and then called Maria again. Still no answer. Now she was worried.

She buzzed Wayne Burrell.

"Yes, Governor, Sgt. Burrell here."

"Wayne, I need to swing by my Mother's house before going to my lunch meeting. You have her address?"

"Yes we do, Governor. We'll have the car in front in five minutes."

The Governor's vehicle – a black Cadillac Escalade SUV – reached Maria's home in ten minutes. Upon exiting the SUV, Wayne immediately noticed the kitchen door hanging by one hinge. He knew what this meant.

"Governor, wait here," Wayne said with authority. Theresa saw the door and didn't object.

One man stayed with Theresa, while Wayne and the third security guard approached the kitchen door with weapons drawn. With his colleague standing to the left of the hanging door, from the right side Wayne quickly peaked twice into the kitchen before entering, immediately followed by the other guard.

"Mrs. Vargas, Mrs. Vargas," Wayne yelled. Upon hearing nothing, Wayne pointed for his colleague to enter the adjoining dining room while Wayne approached the den. Both men found nothing. They searched the remainder of the lower floor before doing the same in the upper floor. Again, no sign of Mrs. Vargas, and no sign of a struggle.

Wayne exited the house and immediately saw the tension on Theresa's face.

"Your mother is not there, Governor."

"She isn't! Did you see any notes or messages?"

"No, nothing. Fortunately, we didn't see any indications of a struggle. I'll call Phoenix PD and have them send some people over here to check for prints. If you approve, they can also put out an APB for your mother. Because she is the parent of the Governor, they'll relax the 24-hour requirement for declaring someone missing."

"Wayne, before you do that, let me call some of my family. Maybe she's with one of them. It's possible the door fell off on its own, and she was worried about being safe. Maybe she went to stay with one of my brothers or my cousin."

Wayne thought this was hopeful thinking on the part of Theresa. To him the scene had all the earmarks of an abduction. But he wouldn't contradict the Governor.

"That's a good idea, Governor."

Since Sophia lived close by, Theresa called her first. Sophia was a late sleeper and sounded groggy, but – no – Maria was not with her.

Theresa next dialed Armando.

"Hello."

"Armando, it's Theresa. Is Momma with you? She's not at home, and her kitchen door looks like it was kicked in."

Armando was silent.

Theresa raised her voice. "Armando, are you there? I'm asking about Momma. Do you know where she is?"

Armando cleared his throat. "Theresa, your call woke me." He spoke with a whisper.

"Armando, I can hardly hear you. Where is Momma?"

"I don't know. I don't know." With that, Armando ended the call.

Last, Theresa called Luis. After fifteen rings her call went to voicemail.

"Luis, this is Theresa. I'm at Momma's house. She's not there and it looks like something bad has happened. Do you know where she is? Do you know what's going on? Call me immediately."

Far away, Luis listened to Theresa's message. He then looked at Maria and wondered what he had done.

"Wayne, she doesn't appear to be with any of my family. Go ahead and call the Phoenix PD."

"Right away, Governor."

"Theresa, Theresa, is that you?"

For a moment Theresa was relieved because she thought it was Maria. Instead, it was one of the neighbors, Frances Hutchens, who was about the same age as Maria and had lived in the neighborhood as long.

They embraced. Theresa was trembling. It had now hit Theresa that her mother might not be alive.

"Mrs. Hutchens, do you know where my mother is?"

"Theresa, I saw her taken away early this morning. It was a big black SUV, just like you have. It was around 6. Several people – I think men – took her out the door and down the stairs and put her in the car. At the time I thought it might have been you and your folks, so I didn't give it much thought."

"But it wasn't me, Mrs. Hutchens, and I didn't send anyone for my Momma. Can you tell me anything else you saw?"

"Well, let me think. Oh, yes. It looked like Maria had some kind of hat on. I thought that was odd, because I don't remember Maria liking to wear hats."

Their discussion was interrupted by a call on Theresa's private cell phone. Her heart jumped, thinking it was one of her family saying her Momma was safe.

She looked at the screen before answering. The caller ID said, 'unknown.'

CHAPTER 21

Phoenix, Arizona and Nogales, Mexico, Thursday, January 6, Late Morning

"Hello, Momma, is this you?" Theresa was hoping the call to her private cell was from Maria. Maybe Maria had rushed to the home of a friend who had become ill. All of Maria's close friends were up in years. Or maybe she took an early morning walk and got tired or disoriented and was calling from a neighbor's home. Maria had a great memory. She would easily remember Theresa's private cell number.

Instead a male voice answered. "No, Governor, this is not your mother, Maria. I'm Miguel. Don't trouble your people to try to find me in your police files, because Miguel is not my real name. Also, we are employing the latest technology to make it impossible to trace this call. But I digress. Maria is right here and she is well and is relaxing."

"Let me talk to her now." Theresa's tone was assertive with twinge of panic.

"Not yet, Governor. You're not the boss here." Theresa's antenna immediately went up. Did that mean Maria was not in Arizona? "You can talk to your mother later. First we have some business to conduct."

Fuentes was using an earbud allowing him to listen to the conversation.

"What kind of business?"

"Here's the situation Governor Vargas. We have something you want – your momma Maria. You have something we want – your support of Concon. The obvious solution is a mutually beneficial trade. You issue a public announcement that, upon serious reflection, you have decided a national Constitutional Convention is in the best interests of the country and the State of Arizona. You will also say you will actively work to persuade your supporters in the legislature to support a Constitutional Convention. Then, when the legislature votes to support the calling of a convention, Maria will be returned to you."

"When will I get my mother back?"

"As I said, when the legislature votes affirmatively for Concon. Oh, sorry, I'm using the shortcut term, but I'm sure you're heard it. And one more thing. The vote has to occur no later than one week from today. You have a week to make your announcement, use your charm on the legislature, and have them vote positively for Concon. When the thumbs-up vote happens by the deadline, you'll get Maria back."

"That's not enough time. You're overstating my powers. Give me a month."

Fuentes shook his head no.

"No can do," replied Miguel. The longer we give you, the more time there is for your bloodhounds to try to find us. And while I'm on that matter, if we see or hear – and we will be watching and listening – that your state police or the feds are searching for Maria, then the deal is off. You'll never see your mother again. Do you understand?"

Theresa felt both anger and fear, but she knew she had to be calm. She also knew she had no options.

"OK, I agree. I'll make an announcement supporting Concon, and I'll do everything I can to have the legislature vote for Concon. This will all be done within a week. Then you promise to send my mother back."

"As long as the vote is yes for Concon. Don't feel sorry for yourself,

Governor. You know people love you, and right now you've got the legislature in the palm of your hand."

Theresa ignored the compliments. "When I complete my end of the bargain, how will I get my mother back?"

"Tsk, tsk, Governor. Good try. Don't worry. You get an affirmative vote on Concon and Maria will be gladly returned to you. The details will come after the vote."

"I want to talk to my mother now. I want to ask her a few questions only she knows the answers to, just in case you really don't have my mother and you're altering someone else's voice."

"Oh, Governor, shots- fired, you've wounded me with your distrust." On the other side of the room, Fuentes had to stifle a laugh. Miguel waited for Fuentes to nod yes. "Sure, you can ask her three secret questions if that will make you feel better."

Miguel pointed to Maria. "Maria, come over her. I have your daughter, the very important Governor of Arizona, who wants to talk to you."

Maria walked over and happily took the phone. Like Fuentes, Miguel used ear buds to listen in.

"Momma, are you OK?"

"Yes, I'm fine, maybe a little tired. They did give me a nice lunch of chicken tacos and tea. Don't worry my sweet Tessa." Tessa was Maria's pet name for Theresa. Both Fuentes and Miguel smiled.

"Momma, I'm going to ask you three questions, and it's important you answer them correctly. Do you understand?"

"Si, si, Tessa."

"Number one, what is your social security number?"

"That's easy." There was a one-second pause. "3." There was a two- second pause. "14." Another two- second pause. "30." Again a two- second pause. "15." Last a one-second pause. "45."

"OK, what's my social security number?"

"Let me think. One-second pause. "2." One-second pause. "70." Two-second pause. "3." Two-second pause. "45." One-second pause. "25." One-second pause. "8."

"Last, what was Daddy's office phone number?"

"I'll never forget that," began Maria. "602." One-second pause. "3." Two-second pause. "97." One-second pause. "0083."

"That's great Momma."

"Tessa, do you want to talk to Luis?"

"Luis?" Is Luis there? Yes, I certainly ...."

Miguel took the phone from Maria and pointed for her to return to the couch. "That's enough family time, Governor. Are you satisfied we have your mother?"

"I am, but is my brother Luis there? Put him on the phone." Miguel looked at Fuentes, who mouthed 'no'.

Miguel ignored Theresa's commands. "We're done here, Governor. You have your instructions. Remember, we'll be watching and listening. Don't disappoint us, but more important, don't disappoint your mother." Miguel ended the call.

Theresa had the security team drive her back to the bungalow. Once there, Theresa laid out the notes she took of Maria's conversation on the dining room table and pulled up a map of southern Arizona on her phone. In between the numbers she had written dashes, with one dash for a one-second pause by Maria and two dashes for a two-second pause. The pauses were important because they represented turns; a one second pause was a right turn, and a two-second pause was a left turn. The numbers in between the pauses were the minutes of driving for that stretch of road.

Decades ago when Theresa had just matured as a teenager, Maria worried about human traffickers. Then it was not uncommon for pretty undocumented women, especially those who spoke English, to be kidnapped and held for ransom or sold for activities Maria didn't even want to consider. Maria devised a coding system Theresa could use to reveal her location without her abductors knowing. It was developed around numeric answers given by the abductee to prove it was her. The system communicated a turn and distance roadmap to a location. Maria and Theresa would take periodic drives to practice the system. Maria made Theresa practice even when she was in college.

When her abductors thought she was asleep on the drive to

the house now holding Maria, her brain was wide awake mentally recording the turns and estimates of driving time. While she feinted simplicity to her captors, Maria was actually a clever and resourceful woman.

Theresa decoded the first social security number:

Right turn from Maria's house, then driving 3 minutes.

Left turn, then driving 14 minutes.

Left turn, then driving 30 minutes.

Left turn, then driving 15 minutes.

Right turn, then driving 45 minutes.

Assuming light traffic leaving Phoenix in the early morning, the first SSN put Maria and the kidnappers driving south on I-10 toward Tucson.

Theresa then decoded the second social security number:

Right and driving for 2 minutes.

Right and driving for 70 minutes.

Left and driving for 3 minutes.

Left and driving for 45 minutes.

Right and driving for 25 minutes.

Right and driving for 8 minutes.

Looking at the map, the kidnappers picked up I-19 south of Tucson and likely crossed the border at Nogales. Theresa assumed they had help at the border.

There were additional rules for the phone number. Since the area code couldn't be faked for a smart criminal, an actual area code given as the first three numbers was ignored. Also, whenever a 9 was used, it and any pauses and numbers after it were ignored as was the pause prior to the 9. So, in the case of 602, pause, 3, double pause, 97, pause, 0084, there was only one more turn:

Right turn and driving for 3 minutes. It was probably a driveway.

Although the system wasn't exact due to variations in speed and estimations of the times, Theresa was sure her mother was being held somewhere in the mountainous area just southwest of Nogales, Mexico.

Taking the kidnappers at their word, Theresa didn't dare involve the state police or the FBI. Fortunately, there was someone close to her whom she could totally trust and could help.

Theresa dialed a number on her private cell.

"Chance of plans? Want to spend the whole day together? I haven't left for the office yet, so that can be arranged."

"Nick, I desperately need your help."

Nick immediately detected the fright in Theresa's tone, something he'd never before heard.

"Of course, anything. What's wrong?"

"Does your firm still have projects in Mexico City?"

"We do."

"I need you to go there, today if possible."

"Certainly, I'll go. What do you want me to do?"

"I need you to save Maria's life."

CHAPTER 22

The Capitol, Washington, DC, Thursday, January 6, Mid Afternoon

CAROL'S PRESS RELEASE WENT VIRAL. EVERY MAJOR NEWS OUTLET picked it up. It was posted and re-tweeted on tens of millions of Facebook and Twitter accounts. Editorials were quickly written about its implications. In a CNN 'breaking news' interview, the Pulitzer Prize winning biographer Jon Meacham seriously intoned, "I don't know if we have a new Revolution, a new Civil War, or both."

Both sides of the Concon debate tried to spin the release to their advantage. Concon supporters used the press release to promote their goal of throwing off the oppressive and ineffective federal government. Concon opponents emphasized the French commentary to play up worries of foreign intervention and boost patriotic feelings for the federal government.

Polls showed the Concon supporters gaining more than the opponents. The upcoming vote in the Senate seemed to be moving in favor of Concon ultimately passing. The latest headcount showed supporters needing only four more affirmative votes for the new 40% rule to be instituted for state legislators to affirm Concon.

Denise finally apologized to Mark for her flirting. She passed it off to the stress of Cooley's murder, the questions of Lt. Evers, and the safety and security she saw in Mark. Their relationship appeared to return to one of Senator/secretary status.

Nursing a modicum of guilt, Mark called Cheryl. He said nothing about Denise. Mark told Cheryl he would make a visit home after the Concon vote. A relief to Mark, Cheryl sounded modestly excited.

Mark continued to be troubled by the comments of the stranger at the Senate subway. However, it had been a couple of days since that encounter, and nothing had appeared to incriminate Mark in any newspaper, website, or social media account. He now thought – and hoped – it was a harmless prank.

"I have a meeting of the Agriculture Committee, and then I should be back around 3," Mark told Denise as he prepared to leave the office. "Remember, if there's any news on the Cooley investigation, text me immediately."

"Will do Senator. See you at 3." Denise gave Mark an enthusiastic wave.

Mark and Joe Ferguson were both members of the Ag Committee and sat next to each other. Today's hearing was on the relative benefits of price supports versus income guarantees for farmers. As a Libertarian, Mark liked neither, but he knew he was in the minority. Four economists were witnesses. Mark had to fight to stay awake during testimonies comprised of endless numbers and constant references to changes in supply and demand. One of his colleagues from Montana actually did fall asleep and then awakened with a loud 'uh.' It was the highlight of the meeting.

"Wow, I'm glad that's over," Joe Ferguson happily stated as he and Mark left the committee room. "I know this stuff is important, but talk about bor-ing. In the good ole days when we were fully funded, I could count on my staff to give me understandable summaries that I could use to make decisions. Now I have to plow through most of the gibberish myself. I guess since you're a numbers guy, it's not that hard."

"Oh, no," countered Mark. "I am a numbers guy, but they're meaningful numbers like revenues, costs, salaries, profits, and taxes. Many of these numbers are theoretical, and I get lost in them."

"That makes me feel better." Joe's background, like most Senators, was in the law. He had been a state judge before being elected to the

U.S. Senate. "And by the way, did you see the British press release about France's take on Concon?"

"Who couldn't see it? It was everywhere I turned."

"Has it changed your view on Concon? Do you still intend to vote no for the easier rules?" Joe asked as the two Senators headed downstairs to the subway that would take them back to their offices.

Like Mark, Joe had expressed opposition to Concon. Mark now wondered if Joe had altered his view.

"I'm still opposed," Mark said as the subway doors opened. "I think Concon is a scheme to let states that have messed up their own economies off the hook. I also think one result of Concon would be to considerably reduce the international power and influence of the U.S., assuming there is still a U.S. after the convention."

"Well, I have to admit, the release has caused me to think some more about my position."

"You're kidding." Mark was surprised because Joe had been even more against Concon than him.

"No, I'm not. I'm not sure we can fix the divisions in the country anymore. Maybe our great 250-year experiment has come to an end. Then there's ...." Joe hesitated in finishing.

"Then there's what." Mark was sure Joe was holding something back.

"Well, a long time ago, about 15 years, I had a DUI conviction. It was public and out-in-the-open, and I've won two statewide elections since then. I thought it was dead and buried. But recently Connie has gotten some mail claiming I was drunk because I was returning from seeing my mistress. She wants to know if it's true."
"Is it?"

"Absolutely not. But it doesn't matter. With today's technology, stuff can easily be made up, and if it's packaged in the right way and sent to the right people, it can kill anyone's political career in a matter of weeks."

Mark was troubled. "So is someone blackmailing you to switch your vote in favor of Concon?"

"The letters to Connie haven't made any reference to the Concon vote, but they still have time. It seems too coincidental to me. First the British press release gins up support for Concon. Then Connie gets the letters. And I'm one of the swing votes that could put Concon over the top. I certainly see a pattern. You have to realize modern politics is no holds – and I mean no holds - barred."

The subway approached the Dirksen Senate Office Building. Joe's office was in the left wing, while Mark's was in the right. They parted and waved.

Joe's apparent blackmail revelation made Mark immediately think again about the stranger's comment to him. Mark wondered if he would be targeted next.

Denise was perky and jovial when Mark entered the office. "How was the meeting, Senator? Were some good decisions made to help our farmers?"

"Huh?" Mark was still thinking about Joe. "Oh, the Ag Committee meeting. No votes were taken. We just heard testimony."

"I'm sure it was good. By the way, this was hand-delivered while you were out." Denise gave Mark a large manila envelope.

"Thanks." Mark quickly retreated into his inner office, afraid of what might be in the envelope. He rapidly opened it.

Mark's fears were confirmed. Inside was an 8 1/2 by 11- inch glossy picture of Denise in her bra straddling Mark sitting in his chair.

"Denise, can you come in here, now."

Denise hurried in. "Yes, Senator."

Mark showed her the photo. "Who took this?"

Denise blanched, opened her mouth, but said nothing. Finally she stammered, "I have no idea."

"Well, someone sure did. Look, here's a note." Mark read it out loud. "This fine picture of our Senator in action will soon find its way to your wife and every newspaper and media outlet in South Carolina –unless – you announce by Sunday you are supporting Concon."

"Senator, honestly I know nothing about this. Please believe me."

There was a loud knock at the outer door. Somewhat relieved, Denise quickly ran out of Mark's office and opened it.

It was Lt. Evers. "Good afternoon, is Senator Williams here?"

Nervously, Denise showed Evers to Mark's office. As Denise started to leave, Evers turned to her, "Ms. Perdue. Please stay. Senator Williams, I've come here to escort Ms. Perdue to my office for questioning."

"I don't understand. I've already told the Senator I had nothing to do with that picture." Denise pointed to the picture in Mark's hand. And how did you find out about it so soon?"

"Picture, what picture?" Evers didn't even look at it. "We need to question you about the murder of Senator Cooley."

CHAPTER 23

Mexico City, Thursday, January 6, Mid Afternoon

Nick caught the 2:30 pm flight direct to Mexico City. He'd always loved the architecture, climate, and people of the "city of palaces." Perched in the Sierra Madre Mountains, most of the city was over half a mile above sea level. The population of almost 9 million enjoyed mild temperatures, low humidity, and limited winters. Smog and crime were the biggest problems in recent decades, but policies of the current president had resulted in notable improvements in both.

Nick packed only an overnight bag, so he was able to grab it from the overhead storage bin and quickly exit the plane when it landed. The Mexico City International Airport, known locally as the Benito Juarez International Airport, was conveniently located to the city but significantly over its capacity. Construction had begun on a new airport, but a previous President – Obrador – had cancelled the project. There was still no resolution to the airport's stifling congestion.

Nick had a small window of opportunity to see his contact, Jorge. Nick brought Theresa's estimate of the location of Maria and her kidnappers. He also brought hope Jorge's associates could find them.

Nick struggled through the throngs of travelers to reach the outside cab platform. After ten minutes he finally secured a ride and was on his way to meet Jorge.

Traffic was always heavy in Mexico City, particularly in the government sector near the center of the city. Nick looked at the

Presidential Palace as they passed. A few blocks later he directed the cabbie to stop.

"Para aquí por favor" (stop here, please), Nick said in perfect Spanish.

The cab halted at a relatively new office building. Nick paid the cabbie, pulled his overnight bag from the back seat, and swiftly walked through the automatic glass doors to the lobby. Looking at the notes he had written, he pressed the button for the third floor. A female office worker returning from lunch also entered the elevator and pushed the five button.

"Buenas tardes" (Good afternoon) Nick said.

The woman gave Nick a quick smile and then resumed looking at her iPhone as the elevator stopped at level three.

Nick again looked at his notes. Room 303. He looked down the hallway and saw it was the first room on the left. Reaching the door, Nick knocked.

The door was opened by an imposing heavily-armed man in a grey suite. Three others like him were also in the room.

"Mr. Phillips?" the man asked in heavily-accented English.

"Yes, I'm Nick Phillips, here to see Jorge."

Nick noticed the man was somewhat taken aback upon hearing the word Jorge.

"Please come this way."

The man led Nick to another door which appeared to be a private office. The man knocked.

"Entrar" (Enter), Nick heard from the other side of the door.

The armed man pushed open the door and stepped aside for Nick to enter.

A short, modestly overweight, balding man in his mid-40s had been using a tablet as he sat on plush upholstered chair. Upon seeing Nick, he immediately jumped up.

"Nicky, it's so great to see you. What has it been, ten years?" The two men gave each other a bear hug.

"At least that, Jorge. Looks like from your waist line life has been good to you."

"I can't complain, Nicky. And if I did, few people would listen."

"Your English is as good as it was at Harvard. Still very little accent."

"And I hear your Spanish isn't bad also. Those were good days at Harvard. I remember them well. Architecture has been good to you, and look at where economics has gotten me."

Nick paused and turned somber. "Gosh, Jorge, it really is good seeing you. But I've got a problem. And it's an even bigger problem for my good friend, the Governor of Arizona, Theresa Vargas."

"So I hear. My people have informed me, but let me hear it from you." Jorge eased back into his chair and pointed to another for Nick.

'Theresa's mother was kidnapped earlier this morning. We think she's being held near Nogales." Nick showed Jorge the location on a map he had brought.

"How do you know this, my friend?" inquired Jorge.

"We know about the kidnapping because the culprits contacted Theresa. Said they would only release Maria – the mother – if Theresa came out in support of a constitutional convention in the U.S. and persuaded the legislature to vote for it. We know the approximate location because Theresa and her mother worked out a code to communicate where Maria was taken."

"Interesting," Jorge stroked a small goatee on his chin. "Mother-daughter relations are amazing. I think my wife and daughter can pass information just by looking at each other."

"Jorge, I have to ask you a touchy question."

"Certainly, go on."

"There's a lot of talk in Arizona that Mexico is supporting the movement for a constitutional convention with an eye to re-taking the western part of the U.S. Some people – but certainly not including me or Governor Vargas – would immediately jump to the conclusion that Maria's kidnapping was helped, if not directed, by Mexico."

"Ah, my good friend, don't be ashamed of asking me that question. I hear the same thing. While there are elements in Mexico that dream of a new Mexican Empire, they are a very small minority. To my knowledge, no one in the Mexican government supports – what's it called – ah, yes – Concon."

Nick exhaled a sign of relief. "I thought that was the case. I'll pass your comments on to Theresa – I mean – the Governor of Arizona."

"I want to meet your Governor. She sounds like a wonderful person and woman. But I take it you know that."

"Yes, she is, and I do. Now, the reason I'm here is to see if you can help secure Maria's release and apprehend the kidnappers."

Jorge said nothing for a moment as he considered Nick's request, again stroking his goatee. "Nick, excuse me a minute. Let me talk to one of my top persons who would know how to handle this matter." Jorge pulled out a cell phone from his suit pocket, dialed a number, and spoke for a few minutes. He referred to Nick's map during the conversation.

Jorge ended the call and looked back at Nick.

"Nick, we'll take care of it. And rest assured, we know how to do these things. We've had plenty of practice. Maria will not be harmed and hopefully will be back with her daughter, the lovely Governor, within a couple of days. We'll do all we can to take the kidnappers alive, but I can't promise that."

Both men rose and shook hands.

"Jorge, thank you so much. I'll pass the good news on to Theresa. You know how to contact me. Please let me know when the operation is done and Maria is safe."

"I will, my friend. Give my regards to the Governor. We'll be talking soon."

There was a soft knock at the door.

Jorge answered. "Entrar."

The same armed man appeared. "Señor. Presidente. El canciller está aquí" (Mr. President. The Foreign Minister is here.)

Jorge had a look of irritation as he turned to Nick. "I don't know how he finds me. It doesn't matter where I hide. And it's always a crisis – in Africa, South America, and even one time in Antarctica. Can you believe it? My Foreign Minister found a crisis in Antarctica that deserved the attention of the President of Mexico."

As he left the office, Nick swung around and said, "It couldn't happen to a better person, Mr. President."

CHAPTER 24

DC Police Headquarters, Washington, DC, Thursday, January 6, Late Afternoon

WITH A DC OFFICER LEADING, LT. EVERS, DENISE, AND MARK left the office and took a now functioning elevator to a waiting police car in the rear of the Capitol. Lt. Evers had consented to Mark's request to accompany Denise to the questioning.

Once reaching the outside, Mark and Denise were surprised to see two police vehicles, with the second already occupied. When they got closer, they could see an anxious looking Darlene sitting in the back seat.

"You're questioning Darlene too?" asked Denise. "Is she also a suspect in Senator Cooley's death?"

Evers held the back door of his car open for Denise and the other officer. He gestured for Mark to sit in the front passenger seat.

"Yes, we are also questioning Ms. Huggins."

"But why, why? We haven't done anything," insisted Denise. "We both adored Senator Cooley."

Evers was unyielding. "We'll discuss all of this at headquarters."

They drove in silence to the DC Metropolitan Police Headquarters building on Indiana Avenue, officially known as the Henry J. Daly Building. Constructed in the 1990s, it was a typical nondescript six story building devoid of any architectural interest or historical significance. Its best feature was its name. Daly was a police sergeant killed in the line of duty.

Evers' office was on the fourth floor. They rode the elevator with again no words spoken. The officers had performed this duty thousands of time. Evers and his colleagues stared ahead at the closed elevator door with a wooden posture. Denise and Darlene nervously fidgeted and looked at the floor. Mark occupied himself by trying to anticipate where Evers' questions might lead. Did he really suspect the twins? Or was he using them to get at the real suspect?

Once in his office, Evers announced the instructions. Ms. Perdue and Ms. Huggins, I will be questioning you separately. If you desire an attorney to be present, now is the time to request one. Do either of you want an attorney?

Denise and Darlene quickly looked at each other and then shook their heads.

"Darlene and I have nothing to hide, and we've done nothing wrong. So, no, we'll answer your questions without an attorney so we can get this over quickly."

Evers made a note. "Alright, I'm indicating both of you have declined having an attorney present. Ms. Perdue, I'll question you first. If you'll please step into this room." Evers pointed to a small windowless room adjoining his office. "Ms. Huggins, once I'm finished with Ms. Perdue, I'll question you next."

Mark spoke up. "Lt. Evers, do you mind if I accompany Ms. Perdue during the questioning? Since this investigation does involve the death of Senator Cooley who, as you know, died in my office, and since Ms. Perdue works for me and was present during the Senator's death, I might save you some time by filling in details Ms. Perdue might not know."

Evers was silent for a few moments while he thought. "Actually, that's not a bad idea. So, yes, Senator Williams, you may sit in on the questioning of Ms. Perdue."

Denise, Mark and Evers entered the room. It was tiny, only maybe 10 by 8 feet. A metal rectangular table and four chairs took up half the space. An electronic device – likely a recorder – was in the center of the table.

Denise sat in a chair on the long side of the table directly across from Evers. Mark sat in a chair on one of the short sides to the right of Denise. An assistant to Evers stood at the door. Evers arranged some notes on the table.

"Ms. Perdue, I will be recording our session, so please speak clearly. This is just a preliminary questioning and you are not charged with anything, so you will not be sworn in. Of course, I expect you to be truthful. Do you understand?"

"Yes, sir, I do understand," Denise responded in her southern drawl, which still perplexed Mark.

"OK, Ms. Perdue, let me start by saying it has been established Senator Cooley was killed by a colorless and odorless poison that was added to the bottle of vodka used to fill her flask."

"That's horrible. I hope she didn't suffer."

"Fortunately, that poison works very fast, so she was killed almost instantly."

Denise showed relief. "Thank God."

Evers continued. "Here's the problem we have. Your fingerprints, as well as those of Ms. Huggins, were found on the vodka bottle in Senator Cooley's apartment."

"My fingerprints. How do you know they're mine?"

"Your fingerprints are on file with the federal government. They were taken when you were appointed to your current job."

Denise thought for a moment. "Oh, that's right. I remember now."

Observing Denise, Mark thought she didn't show sufficient concern about the implications of her fingerprints being on the bottle that apparently filled Bee's flask.

"The point is, Ms. Perdue, your fingerprints are effectively on part of the murder weapon. The other part is the poison, which I expect the killer wouldn't leave lying around in Senator Cooley's apartment. Can you explain how your prints got on the vodka bottle?"

"I can, and I'm not proud of it. It must have been a couple of days before Senator Cooley's death. Darlene called me to say the Senator was out-of-town at a conference. Darlene has a key to the Senator's apartment so she can get her mail, water plants, and make sure everything is fine when the Senator is gone."

Denise paused. "Could I have a glass of water?"

"Jenkins, get Ms. Perdue a glass of water." Jenkins quickly returned with a paper cup of water from a cooler. Denise took a sip.

"Please continue, Ms. Perdue."

"Well, Darlene asked me to go with her to Senator Cooley's apartment to, sort-of, take a break. This was before Senator Williams arrived, so things were slow in the office. We thought we'd relax for a while. We looked in the refrigerator and saw there was a newly opened bottle of vodka. We both poured ourselves a little glass and talked."

"That's it?"

"Yes, Lt. Evers, that's it. We washed and cleaned the glasses and put them back in the cabinet. We put the mail on the dining room table, tidied up, and left."

"You didn't wipe the vodka bottle?" queried Evers.

Denise looked puzzled. "No, why should we have? We took care of the glasses because we didn't want Senator Cooley to know we used them. We didn't drink much vodka, so we didn't think the Senator would notice. We never thought about our fingerprints on the bottle."

Mark addressed Evers. "Lieutenant, were Denise and Darlene's prints on the flask?"

Evers looked annoyed by the interruption, but still answered. "No, they weren't."

Mark continued. "Were there prints other than Senator Cooley's on the flask?"

Evers gave Mark a hard stare." "I'm not at liberty to say now."

Mark had one more question. "Lieutenant, if Denise and Darlene did put the poison in Senator Cooley's flask and had the presence of mind to wipe the flask clean, wouldn't they have done the same to the vodka bottle?"

Evers ignored Mark and pressed on with Denise.

"Ms. Perdue, you say you were born in South Carolina, correct?"

"Oh, yes, I'm a proud Palmetto." Denise seemed to emphasize her drawl.

"Then why can't we find a birth certificate for you in South Carolina's records?"

"Maybe that's because Perdue is my married name. I kept it even though I'm divorced."

"We know that. On your federal job application, you wrote your maiden name was Graham. We can only find one South Carolina birth certificate for Denise Graham, and she was born in 1907. I know you're not that old." Evers issued the last statement with a confident grin.

Denise's cooperative attitude suddenly changed. "That's all I'm going to say. Anything else will be said in the presence of my attorney."

Denise folded her arms and looked at the door. It was an amazing transformation. Denise went from being charming and innocent to steely-eyed and protective. Even more amazing, her voice changed from southern drawl to high-brow English.

CHAPTER 25

The British Embassy, Washington, DC, Friday, January 7, Mid Morning

ALTHOUGH IT WAS ONLY THE DAY AFTER SETTING THE RECORD FOR the top number of media hits for - what had been dubbed – the 'French Connection' press release, Carol was being viewed almost like royalty in the Embassy. When passing colleagues in the hall, everyone gave her a smile and thumbs-up congratulations. Natalie told Carol she would now consult her on almost every release, even those not written by Carol. There were rumors Carol's work had drawn the attention of the Ambassador, who may have bigger plans for the girl wonder. But most important, Carol was told she would be receiving a nice pay raise. This would allow her and Tony to pay off the loan on the car they had just purchased months in advance.

Although she has only been in Washington a few days, Carol was enjoying the city. As an historian, she avidly followed the constant rancor and drama taking place daily in Congress. She wondered what the legislative giants of the past, like Webster, Rayburn, and even Lyndon Johnson, would have thought. Could Johnson have been able to use his powers of personal persuasion combined with knowledge of legislators' vulnerabilities to establish some semblance of order? She thought not.

What worried Carol most about the current political climate was Concon. Although her academic focus had been British history, Carol had closely studied the founding of the United States and the creation of the Constitution. Among the world's major political documents, she thought the U.S. Constitution was the best. It carefully balanced the rights of individuals and the differences between states with the need for a central authority having limited powers. Its predecessor, the Articles of Confederation, showed that without a strong, but controlled, central government, there would be no bond between the states to resist foreign interference and ultimate domination. States would be individually picked off like pigeons on a roost.

Natalie handed Carol a pile of papers including articles to be written as press releases and reports to edit.

"If this is too much, just let me know." Carol's success had also heightened Natalie's status within the Embassy, and Natalie didn't want to lose her star worker.

"Don't worry. This looks manageable. Plus, I actually enjoy reading the material."

Before turning to other desks, Natalie added, "I know I won't be able to keep you long. You're destined to go places."

Carol's morning was uneventful. She wrote a press release about the Ambassador attending a meeting at the White House to plan a visit by the UK Prime Minister. There was a second highlighting a recent expansion of a British apparel firm in Tennessee.

After a quick lunch with Tony, Carol continued to make her way through the stack of work. A third of the way down the pile Carol came upon a thick report, probably thirty pages in length. This will take the rest of the afternoon, she thought. Then she saw the title – 'The British Empires.' Carol wondered if there was a typo in the last word. She knew of only one British Empire – one spanning the 16th thru the first half of the 20th centuries and stretching around the world. It spawned the phrase, 'the sun never sits on the British Empire.'

The report looked like a high-level policy paper. Carol had never received one like it before. Maybe with her new status and background in British history, the higher-ups wanted her feedback on both style and content. Carol considered showing Natalie the report to make sure she hadn't received it by mistake, but her curiosity beat out her caution.

Carol liked to read reports all the way through before doing editing. The report had four sections. The first gave background on the only British Empire she knew of over 200 years ago, that included regions like the British Isles, Egypt, India, Canada, south and east Africa, Hong Kong, Australia, and – for a while – the thirteen American colonies. Carol thought the authors placed too little emphasis on Malaya and Singapore being a key strategic links between Britain's western and eastern territories.

The second section documented the collapse of the Empire after World War II. The report pointed to Britain's financial bankruptcy from two world wars as the main cause, and Carol agreed. It reaffirmed for Carol the lesson that countries winning wars do not always win the peace.

Carol yawned. Thus far the report read like a freshman text in world history, and an average one at that. She wondered why it was written. Carol was rapidly losing interest and didn't look forward to the changes she'd recommend to make the writing more readable.

Carol's attitude quickly changed when she began reading the third section. It focused on the geo-political changes occurring in recent decades and how they impacted the UK. The biggest change was the demise of the European Union (EU) and the formation of smaller alliances in Europe. Also significant were the end of Russia as a world power due to declining population, civil strife in China as the Communist Party tried to prevent power shifting to the growing democracy movement, and the rise of India as the prominent economy in the Far East. Half the section was also devoted to the disintegration of a functioning political system in the U.S. and the growing calls for a new constitutional convention.

The fourth and final section was the shocker. It outlined the formation of a new British Empire to dominate the world. It would include the UK and her current allies in Europe – mainly Scandinavia and the Low Countries – and would add countries from the original empire such as Egypt, India, Australia, and Canada. The report indicated preliminary talks had already begun with these countries and had progressed positively. An important difference between the old and new empire would be political representation from all regions on an Empire Council. Yet like the original empire, the nominal head of the new empire would be the British monarch. It was envisioned the revived British Empire would control the major commercial routes and financial transactions in the world.

But there was more. Plans for the second British Empire included incorporating the Northeastern and Midwestern states of the U.S. Although these regions were struggling economically, they still had substantial financial and corporate assets in New York City and Boston, as well as manufacturing assets along the Great Lakes. The plan foresaw coordinating low-cost labor in India and Africa with capital and technology from Canada and the U.S. acquisitions. The goal would be to develop a juggernaut of economic power that no country or region in the world could overcome.

Carol stopped. She couldn't believe what she had just read. She so wanted to vent with someone, but she knew she couldn't do it here. Even though it was obvious she was mistakenly given this top-secret report, it would likely mean her job – and maybe more – if anyone knew.

The final pages of the report increased Carol's fears to an even higher level. They detailed the steps the British were taking to create political disarray in the U.S. The goal was to stir support for a constitutional convention which would culminate in a fatally weakened federal government. States would effectively become independent, thereby enabling the British to offer sweetheart deals for states they coveted to join the new British Empire.

The British were using two tactics to pursue their goals. First was information control. The *Le Monde* article that Carol unwittingly made viral was a British fake, created by British agents who infiltrated the French Foreign Ministry and passed false information to the media. By characterizing the Concon movement as an uprising against an oppressive federal government, the British wanted to give added momentum to the movement. Also, the story of a French-Spanish plot to form a new Mexican Empire including much of the American west was phony. It was designed to rev-up feelings of glory held by some Hispanic-Americans who would then also support Concon. Other disinformation offensives were planned.

The second tactic was a political offensive through blackmail and other means. Selected politicians, especially in states not yet supporting Concon, would be targeting for "persuading" – the word was actually in quotes. Examples were not given for the form of the persuasion, but Carol could imagine.

Carol was shaking. She now considered everyone in the Embassy her enemy. She saw deceit and danger in her colleague's eyes. She needed a plan - for herself, Tony, and, especially, for the country – before it was too late.

CHAPTER 26

The British Embassy, Washington, DC, Friday, January 7, Late Afternoon

CAROL NEEDED A WAY TO GET THE EMPIRE DOCUMENT OUT OF THE Embassy. No one would believe what Carol read in the report. Only releasing the report to the media would be proof of the British plans. If she was caught stealing the document, Carol could face jail. But with patriotism overcoming her, she had to try.

It was 5:15. Natalie walked through the media room and saw Carol still working. Carol had hidden the empire report in her desk drawer.

"Don't stay too long. Remember, we don't pay you overtime, but I do hope that salary bump showed you how much we value your work."

Carol was relieved Natalie didn't ask about the empire report. Apparently, she didn't know Carol had it. If Natalie had asked, Carol would have played dump.

"Oh, I don't have much longer," Carol responded. "I got caught up in this British apparel company expansion in Tennessee. Did you know the company has been around for 200 years? Started in England, then migrated to the New England states in the 1700s, and then to Tennessee in the late 1800s."

"I didn't know that. That's great context for the press release. This is a good example of how important your historical perspective is. Well, I'm out of here. Too-da-loo, as we British say. See you tomorrow."

"Have a great evening, Natalie." With any luck, Carol would never see Natalie again.

As Natalie walked down the hall she was sure Carol saw and read the empire report she secretly had placed in Carol's stack. The question now was, would Carol use it the way Natalie wanted?

Carol was in the media room by herself. She had to think fast. How could she get the report out of the Embassy without being caught? Carol knew Embassy documents had an invisible scanner tag that would set off an alarm at each of the round-the-clock exit checkpoints in the Embassy. This was to prevent sensitive material from inadvertently – or purposefully – leaving the building. Even copies of documents carried the tag. Carol was also sure windows had been fitted with alarms to prevent unauthorized opening.

There was one possibility that could work. In her orientation tour of the floor, she was shown a utility room which included staff bathrooms. But the room also included a washer and dryer. The washer and dryer were used to clean tablecloths and napkins from the nearby banquet room.

Dryers – at least the ones she knew – had to be vented to release the hot air generated during the drying process. If she could move the dryer and access the vent, then the report could be pushed through the vent to the outside. Carol and Tony could then retrieve it before anyone was aware. Also, for personal privacy reasons, there were no security cameras in the utility room.

Carol dialed Tony. He typically lost track of time when he was absorbed in a project. Tony immediately answered.

"Hey, sweetie. He glanced at the nearby clock. Oh, no, it's almost 5:30. Where's my head? I'll close things down here and then meet you at the main entrance in, say, ten minutes."

Even though no one was around, Carol couldn't help but whisper. "No, make it 45 minutes, at 6:15. It should be dark then."

Tony was surprised by Carol's answer. "OK. I guess you're in the middle of something also."

Carol again spoke in a hushed tone. "You could say that. I'll explain later. Just remember, 6:15 out front. Don't get lost in your work and forget."

"I won't. See you then." Tony noticed the seriousness in Carol's voice and was concerned.

Carol pulled the empire report from her desk drawer and headed to the utility room. The hallway was dark and she seemed to be alone. Carol opened the door to the utility room, quickly closed it, and flipped on the light switch. The washer and dryer were in an alcove just wide enough to accommodate the two appliances. Carol would have to pull the dryer out just enough to allow her to climb over the washer and drop behind the dryer. Fortunately, she wore slacks today.

Carol folded the report and stuffed it under her belt. She then grabbed both sides of the dryer and slowly inched it out with a gentle rocking motion. After each pull she stopped to listen for any nearby noise. She heard none. She stopped when the dryer was about two feet away from the outside wall.

Carol then lifted herself on top of the washer, scooted a few inches to the back of the machine, and then slowly dropped herself behind the dryer. When she and Tony recently installed a dryer in their New York home, she remembered the instructions said to connect the vent tube to the dryer with duct tape rather than screws. Apparently, there was an issue with sparks possibly being emitted from the screws as the warm air moved over them, possibly resulting in a fire. When she pulled out the dryer, the duct tape was loosened and the dryer was disconnected from the vent tube, thus leaving a clear passage through the wall. Carol removed the report from under her belt, rounded the report to have a circumference smaller than the vent, and pushed it through the vent. Success!

Before Carol could climb back over the washer, she heard a knock at the door.

"Security. Just checking since I see the light is on. Is anyone in there? If so, state your name and position."

Carol stopped. "This is Carol Shipman. I'm an editor in the media room. Give me a couple of minutes and I'll be done."

"OK Ms. Shipman. I'll check your ID when you come out. Regulations you know."

Carol heard the guard move away. Even so, she couldn't risk the noise of pushing the dryer back in its place. This meant as soon as the report was discovered missing, there would be no doubt how it was removed from the building.

Carol ran the sink at full blast, washed her hands, and emerged still wiping them with paper towels.

"Here I am," Carol cheerfully said to the guard after closing the door behind her. "My ID is at my desk in the media room." Carol wanted to immediately move the guard away from the utility room and the displaced dryer.

The guard followed Carol to her desk where she pulled her Embassy ID card from her purse. Fortunately, Carol had left the lights on in the media room so it looked like she had just stepped away to use the bathroom.

The guard studied the ID and returned it to Carol. "Working late?"

"Oh, yes. I had a lot of catching-up to do," answered Carol.

"But I don't see any work on your desk, and your computer is turned off."

Did the guard suspect something, wondered Carol? She now wished she'd told Tony to meet her inside at the media room.

Despite her nervousness, Carol tried to sound calm and matter-of-fact. "That's because I just finished. I needed to use the lady's room before meeting my husband outside. He also works for the Embassy in the other building."

Carol's mention of Tony and the fact he was also an Embassy employee seemed to mollify the guard.

"Have a good evening, ma'am." The guard tipped his hat and returned to the hallway.

Carol was scared and couldn't wait to see Tony. She guessed the guard would soon be checking the utility room. Carol put on her coat, slung her purse strap over her shoulder, smiled politely to the security person at the exit scanner, and breathed a sigh of relief as she left the building and saw Tony waiting.

"You're late," Tony jovially said upon seeing Carol exit the Embassy. "I think that's a first. It's usually me that's late."

"Tony, we have to hurry, but not too much. If there are any guards outside, we don't want to attract attention. Walk fast, but don't run, and follow me." Carol was headed around the side of the building to the dryer vent hole.

"OK, I'm coming." Carol's speed surprised Tony. "What's going on?"

"I can't tell you now. Good, there it is." Carol pointed to the dryer vent hole in the wall.

"There what is? I don't see anything." Tony was getting tired of what appeared to him to be a game.

"The hole through the wall for the dryer vent." Carol was already at the spot. She bent down, reached through the hole, removed the empire report, and stuffed it in her oversized purse. "OK, now let's walk nonchalantly to the car."

"Will you please …."

Carol interrupted Tony before he could finish his sentence. 'Tony, look. There's a flashlight headed our way. I'm sure it's a guard. Let me do the talking."

Exasperated, Tony answered, "I certainly will, since I don't know what we're doing."

Upon reaching them, the guard, a middle-age man with salt and pepper curly hair, illuminated Carol and Tony's faces with his flashlight.

"May I ask what the two of you were doing near the Embassy?"

"Oh, we're employees of the Embassy." Carol already had her ID card out and she nudged Tony to do the same." The guard examined the cards, and satisfied, returned them.

"Fine, so you work for the Embassy. But what were you doing over there? I saw one of you squatting down and apparently looking for something."

Carol giggled. "Yeah, I can explain. I lost one of my earrings during a luncheon in the banquet hall. I was worried it may have gotten wrapped up with the linens and washed. You know there's a laundry room right there on the first floor. And I thought my earring may have come out the dryer vent, so that's what I was checking."

The guard looked unsure. "Interesting. If what you say is true, I would think the earring would still be in the washer, or if it was in the dryer, it would be in the lint tray."

"Oh, I checked both of those, and no luck. So that's why I wanted to check outside." Carol was tightly squeezing Tony's hand to help with her nervousness.

"Alright, that makes sense," replied the guard. Carol was relieved until he continued. "But I don't see an earring on your other ear."

"Ha, I can tell you don't know about women's fashion, at least the fashion I like. I never wear one earring. I always wear them in a set. So, when I missed one, I immediately removed the other." Carol was almost holding her breadth that the guard didn't ask to see the earring.

"I suggest you talk to the cleaning staff and check other places for your missing earring. And please don't lurk around the building after dark again. We wouldn't want you mistaken for prowlers or burglars. Have a good evening." With that the guard continued on his route.

Once they were removed from the guard's earshot, Tony couldn't contain himself.

"Now what was THAT all about? Are you going all Jane Bond on me?"

"In a way, yes. But rather than working to save the British Empire, I'm trying to prevent it."

CHAPTER 27

The British Embassy, Washington, DC, Friday, January 7, Late Evening

Denise and Darlene sat in the MI6 attaché's office in the British Embassy. When the Embassy's attorney had arrived at Evers' office the previous day, he admitted Denise and Darlene were British agents, and as such, they enjoyed diplomatic immunity. There was nothing Evers could do other than require the twins leave the country within 48 hours.

"Our cover is broken," began Denise with no attempt at a Southern accent. "Too bad. I enjoyed working here. I especially enjoyed perfecting that Southern accent."

The MI6 officer – Wellesley – laughed. "You both had me fooled. You sounded as Southern as Vivian Leigh in *Gone with the Wind*."

"It was those damn fingerprints on the witch's vodka bottle," exclaimed Darlene. "That led Evers to check our names and birthplaces. However, I'll tell you one thing. I won't miss working for the Queen, her holiness Cooley. You should have seen how people fawned over her. The only good thing about being around her was occasionally seeing her hot-to-trot ex-husband. I will miss him."

"Watch your hormones, Daphne."

"Since we're dropping our fake names, Pricilla, I've seen you check out his rear."

"OK, OK, ladies," intervened Wellesley. "The big question is what we're going to do with you. You know you have to be out of the country by tomorrow."

"Yeah, yeah, we know," admitted Pricilla. "Still, it isn't fair. We didn't have anything to do with killing old lady Cooley." Daphne nodded in agreement. "Why would we kill her? We had a good cover going and had access to all sorts of information and" – Pricilla was smiling now – "good-looking Senators."

Wellesley had already decided what to do. "We have you two booked on a ride in the Embassy van to Toronto tomorrow. It's easier than trying to fly you out of the country and getting by TSA. The Yanks could make it tough for you to pass security. At the Canadian border our people will quickly check you through."

"A van ride. Why can't we take a direct flight to London?" protested Daphne.

Wellesley shook his head no. "We do have a budget, and flying you two back to England is not in it. You'll be debriefed in Toronto and then a decision will be made what to do with you." With a slight smile, Wellesley added, "Quite frankly, getting yourselves implicated in Cooley's murder was not a good thing. That was dumb thinking to help yourselves to her vodka, and in her apartment no less. Many a couple of months of secretarial work is in your future."

Daphne and Pricilla weren't happy, but they couldn't disagree.

"Is that all? We need a little time to gather our things and say goodbye to this wonderful city before the grueling seven-hour van ride."

"Yes, that's all." Wellesley dismissed them with a wave and then resumed looking at some papers on his desk. Just as the twins reached the door, he interrupted them.

"By the way, you'll have some company on the trip."

Daphne and Pricilla stopped and turned. "We will, who?" Pricilla asked.

"Natalia Tewkesbury."

"Tewkesbury? Is she being banished too?" asked Daphne.

"Yes, she is. I'm pretty sure she'll eventually be sent back to

England and kicked out of the service. She may even be tried for treason."

"Why, what did she do? asked the twins almost in unison.

"She gave a top secret report documenting our plans in North America to an American working here. And now that American has disappeared, with the report."

Daphne and Pricilla looked at each other. "That's not good," the latter responded. "So, our cover would have been blown anyway if that report gets into the wrong hands."

Wellesley rose from his desk, walked to a window, and stared out. "That's the least of our worries."

The twins took that as an indication to leave. Daphne walked out, but Pricilla stopped and asked one last question.

"Any idea why Tewkesbury did it?"

Wellesley answered without turning around. "She said something about loving the United States of America."

Wellesley had a busy evening. After the twins left he met with his staff.

"Her name is Carol Shipman, and she's married to Tony Shipman, who has also worked at the Embassy in the new tech center next door," explained the Embassy intelligence agent.

"Do we know where they are now?" asked Wellesley.

"Our last contact with them was a few hours ago when a night security guard found them lurking outside the Embassy. We now know the girl slipped the report through the dryer vent on the first floor."

"That's very clever," Wellesley admitted. "Have we sent agents to their residence?"

"Yes, we sent personnel to their apartment but they were not there," answered the agent.

"Did they enter the apartment?" queried Wellesley.

"Yes, they did. It looked as though the Shipman's had left quickly."

"Do we have the specs on their car?"

"Yes, we do."

"Do we have their cell phone numbers?"

"Yes, we do."

"Can we put locational trackers on those numbers?"

"Yes, we can. We are waiting for your authorization."

Wellesley paused. He was again sitting at his desk. As he often did when in deep thought, he rocked back and looked up at the ceiling. After he reached a decision, he brought his chair back to the sitting position and faced the agent.

"The next steps are serious, but this is a serious situation. Dispatch two units to find and follow the Americans. Employ the usual precautions. Tell the units to hang back. We only want surveillance now. Have the units report directly to me hourly. Only on my command will further action be authorized. Is that clear?"

"Yes, sir, it is."

Wellesley dismissed the agent and resumed his contemplative position. There was a lot riding on the next 24 to 48 hours – his reputation, the reputation of the Ambassador - who would get the credit or blame for whatever happened - and the integrity of the British Foreign Service.

Yet most importantly the next 24 to 48 hours could determine if there would be a Second British Empire.

CHAPTER 28

Washington, DC, Friday, January 7, Late Evening

Carol and Tony's last hours in Washington had been a blur. On the way to their apartment Carol had brought Tony up to speed on the report and her decision to steal it. Tony couldn't believe what Carol was saying. Since his birthday was near, at one point he thought she was playing a joke. But her emphatic responses convinced him she was dead serious.

They had both agreed to leave Washington immediately. Before they reached the apartment, they stopped at an ATM and removed all the cash they had. They packed in record time and were in their new car – a 15-year-old BMW with 175,000 miles – in thirty minutes. They didn't worry about the lease. The landlord would have no trouble renting the unit.

The couple designed a plan as they drove. Goal one was just to leave the city. Carol knew it wouldn't take the British long to realize the report was missing. She guessed they'd stop at little to get it back.

But where should they go; where would they be safe? Carol's inclination was to hide. Tony had another idea.

Tony drove the BMW over the Memorial Bridge to Arlington, being careful to stay under the speed limit. He thought there was the possibility the British could have convinced the DC police they were thieves – which of course, they were. Then his brain latched on to what he thought was the perfect strategy.

"You've heard the phrase; the best defense is a good offense?"

"Of course, that was Mao's strategy in the Chinese civil war." Carol responded, rather irritated. She wondered if Tony was trying to distract her with silly jokes or puzzles.

"Well, that's exactly what we need to do. We need to take the offense."

Tony was silent for a couple of minutes while he maneuvered the BMW onto I-95, which was always a parking lot almost any time of day. At least as they crept along, he felt free to talk.

"We need to go on the offense by getting this report publicized. Once the word is out about what the Brits are up to, they'll be on the defensive. They'll forget about us as the full weight of the U.S. government and the press comes down on them. We won't matter at all."

Carol was intrigued. "That's actually a great idea. But here's the flaw. No one will believe us. We're nobody. Even if we show press people the report, they won't think it's real. They'll assume we wrote it to get our 30 seconds of fame in this crazy world of instant celebrities. We may even be arrested and then sued by the British. Wouldn't that be ironic?"

"I've thought of that, my love." The BMW was inching ahead at only 10 miles per hour. "We need to convince someone who is thoughtful, willing to listen, and who still has enormous credibility. We'll then let that person go on the offense for us."

"You don't mean ..?"

"Yes, I do mean," Tony answered before Carol could finish. "Warren Strom."

Three car lengths behind Carol and Tony was a nondescript blue Ford Taurus with two MI6 agents inside. Anticipating that Carol and Tony might get tired of the traffic congestion, a similar vehicle – this one grey – was parked in a fast food lot near the next exit.

The lead agent in the trailing vehicle – Barker – checked in with Wellesley.

"They're on I-95 heading south and are just north of the route

236 exit. Smiley and Brooke are posted at that exit in case they turn off, which I expect they will."

"Good. Keep tracking them. Based on what they do, we'll plan our intervention," Wellesley responded.

"Yes, sir. I'll update you in another hour unless something changes."

Warren Strom was a broadcasting legend. He began in news at a small rural radio station in Virginia when he was only 17. His deep voice, precise diction, and folksy whit endeared him to audiences and propelled a rapid ascent in the medium. By age 25 he was the lead radio newscaster for ABC. Strom shunned offers to jump to television. He didn't think he had the appropriate looks, and he also didn't like the way TV news was changing. When cable and then the internet caused the media to fragment, and when the FCC eliminated the fairness doctrine for broadcasters, Strom saw news programs becoming more opinionated and melodramatic. Rather than sticking to facts and analysis, anchors and reporters became agents for particular points of view on the political spectrum. They also looked for the smallest foible or mistake to blow up into a spectacular crisis worthy of 'breaking news.' The changes reflected the divisions of the American public into warring tribal camps and a collapsing attention span needing constant sensationalism to be awakened.

Strom didn't change, and as a result he became a media dinosaur. First ABC fired him. Afterward, Strom didn't last long at the several major media markets where he landed. Even small local stations, like the one that gave him his start, didn't want him. It was all because Warren Strom continued to deliver the news the way he always did – present the facts and provide analysis offering all points of view.

Despite largely being ignored, Warren Strom continued to broadcast three days a week from his home in Lynchburg, Virginia using an obscure satellite channel. He had a loyal following, although too small for any major advertiser to care. Now in his 70s, Strom survived on his IRAs, contributions from listeners, and one advertiser who stuck with him – Jack and Jill's Custom-Made Birdhouses.

Carol's brain immediately considered the negatives of Tony's idea. "Do you think Mr. Strom will believe our story?"

"We can only try," answered Tony, who was the optimist of the two. "We really have nothing to lose. Lynchburg is just a minor detour from heading straight to Raleigh. Plus, if we are being followed, the back roads of Virginia will give us more opportunity to lose our pursuers."

"If we're headed to Lynchburg, let's get off 95." Carol pointed to a road sign they were about to pass. "Look, the exit for route 236 is coming up. We can take it over to 29 and then make a direct shot to Lynchburg. This is the way Dad would take us on our camping trips in the Shenandoah Valley."

"At least those camping trips have proven to be good for something," Tony joked. He wasn't a fan of camping. Despite their limited income, 'roughing it' for Tony meant staying in anything less than a four-star hotel.

"Speaking of camping, it's now 9," Carol observed after looking at the clock on her smart phone. If we keep going we won't reach Lynchburg until after midnight, obviously too late to see Mr. Strom. I'm drained. Let's drive as far as Manassas and find a place to stay. On our trips to Virginia Dad would take us to the nearby Civil War battlefields. There are plenty of inexpensive motels."

"Inexpensive means less than four-star," responded Tony. "But you're our planner." Carol gave Tony a playful poke.

Their well-travelled BMW sped along the lightly used highway in the dark of the evening.

"You know, this hasn't been so bad," Carol observed. Carol looked out the back window. "I haven't seen any suspicious cars. We might just pull this off."

In under an hour they were in Manassas and found a Comfort Inn. Carol and Tony checked in and looked forward to a sound sleep.

"They've just stopped at a motel, my guess is for the evening," reported Barker to Wellesley.

"Perfect," replied the MI6 chief.

"Shall we execute the plan?" asked Barker.

"Affirmative. Executive Plan Prevent."

Wellesley again assumed the contemplative position behind his desk. He was pleased. If Plan Prevent worked as expected, by this time tomorrow the report will have been recovered and the thieves neutralized. He would be a hero in the Embassy, with a likely promotion as a reward.

CHAPTER 29

Manassas, Virginia, Saturday, January 8, Early Morning

CAROL AND TONY WERE ASLEEP ALMOST AS SOON AS THEIR HEADS hit their pillows. They were both physically and emotionally exhausted. Although they had escaped danger today, there was no guarantee the same would happen tomorrow. They planned to rise early and get on the road for – what they hoped – was an uneventful trip to Lynchburg.

The two MI6 cars were parked in the farthest corner of the Comfort Inn lot, purposefully away from the overhead lights. The four agents would divide into three teams. One would stay with the cars and the transmitters to the Embassy in case of an emergency. A second was assigned to Carol and Tony's car. The remaining two would perform the needed operation in Carol and Tony's room.

The Comfort Inn couldn't have been better arranged for the tasks the MI6 teams would perform. The inn was a two-level structure with rooms all accessed from the outside. Lower level rooms were entered from the parking lot, and upper level rooms from a second story walkway. Carol and Tony's room was on the lower level in the rear of the building and away from the lobby entrance. The setup was perfect for the agents.

It was 2 am, long enough for the targets to be sound asleep. There was no activity in the parking lot. Even the lobby showed only one dim light. The MI6 team split up and went to work.

The agent assigned to the Embassy vehicles contacted Wellesley.

With such a high priority operation, Wellesley was foregoing sleep to keep up-to-date on the progress. The agent informed Wellesley the operation was in motion.

The agent assigned to Carol and Ted's BMW approached the vehicle with a tiny hand-held mechanism. Holding it next to any lock would immediately open the lock. There would be no signs of forced entry or even remnants of metal contact.

The agent opened the passenger side rear door and placed the package under the front passenger seat. It used to be common for such packages to be hidden in the trunk. Eventually this led transporters to use less-common hiding places, and the underneath of the front passenger seat was today at the top of that list.

The most important, and potentially dangerous, task was the one carried out by the two agents who were about to enter Carol and Ted's room. Dressed completely in black including black body paint on their faces, the two agents used the same hand-held mechanism to silently enter the room. Carol and Tony were asleep, gently snoring. An agent approached each and carefully placed a cloth soaked with Rohypnol over their nose and mouth. This assured the agents Carol and Tony would not awaken for at least an hour.

Using small flashlights, the agents systematically went through the couple's luggage. It didn't take one of the agents long to whisper "I've got it" when he recognized the cover of the British Empire report. He stuffed the report into an inside jacket pocket. Then both agents retraced their steps and rejoined their colleagues at the cars. Wellesley was immediately notified with the simple message, 'Plan Prevent successful.' The agents split into the two cars, slowly pulled out of the parking lot, and began their trip back to Washington.

On the way the MI6 team did have one more task to accomplish. An agent phoned the Virginia State Police to be on the lookout for a couple he observed doing a drug deal in a motel parking lot. And yes, the caller said, he did have the vehicle's description and license plate number.

A few hours later both Carol and Ted awakened with strong

headaches. They noticed their luggage had been moved. Carol looked through their clothes and saw the report was gone. She was happy.

"They took the bait," she told Tony, pointing to the part of her suitcase where the report had been stored.

"Ah, yes," Tony agreed. "You were right that we'd probably get a visit from the spies from across the pond. It's creepy they were in our room, and I don't enjoy the headache, but we did fool them. Thinking ahead and copying the first page of the report before you pushed it through the dryer vent was brilliant. And you were right again in expecting they would not look at any pages beyond the initial one."

"Wait until the MI6 boss sees the other pages are just copies of my press releases," smiled Carol. "And while we're passing out compliments, your idea from the movie *The French Connection* for hiding the real report was also brilliant. Did you get that idea from my viral press release being called *The French Connection?*"

"Maybe so. That scene of Gene Hackman's character, Popeye, saying to the mechanic, 'Lou, you took this car completely apart, didn't you?', and Lou replying, 'Sure, everything except the rocker panels' is one of my favorites. And, of course, Lou found the cocaine hidden in the rocker panels. Hiding the real report in one of the BMW rocker panels is sort of my version of *The French Connection*."

Carol and Tony were packing while they were talking. "OK, I think we're set," Carol observed. "Let's get going and pick up some breakfast later. My guess is the MI6 boss is just about now realizing he doesn't have the real report. But when we get to Lynchburg in a couple of hours we'll have a six-hour lead over them."

They stopped at a combination gas station and McDonald's in Lovingston and ordered egg McMuffins and coffee after they gassed up.

They were now back on 29 headed south. "Look, only 38 miles to Lynchburg," Carol said as she pointed to a sign. "I looked up the phone number for Mr. Strom, so we can call him when we get to the city."

Just then the couple heard a siren. It was a Virginia state trooper right at their bumper.

"Were you speeding?" Carol asked looking at Tony.

"Not at all. I've actually been running a little under the speed limit."

The trooper approached the car with his hand on the butt of his revolver. The name on his tag was Barclay.

"Both of you step out of the vehicle." His tone indicated he meant business.

Carol and Tony complied. "Officer, I don't think we were speeding."

The trooper ignored Tony and spoke into his collar speaker. "Unit 56 at mile marker 265 on Highway 29 requests backup. Possible drug possession." He listened. "OK, 10-4."

Carol spoke up. "Drug possession! We don't have any drugs. We've never used drugs."

The trooper had relaxed. Carol and Tony didn't look threatening. "Ma'am, we received a report. We have to follow through on it. I need to wait for my backup before commencing a search."

Carol and Tony were shocked, but decided the best approach was to remain silent.

In ten minutes another trooper pulled up. She and Barclay conferred. Barclay stepped over to Carol and Tony.

"Trooper Owens will now conduct a search of your vehicle based on probable cause. Do you understand?"

Both Carol and Tony nodded. But Carol couldn't restrain herself. "You won't find anything."

Trooper Owens checked the front seat area including the glove compartment. Then she moved to the back seat and looked under the drivers' seat. Next, she moved around to the passenger side and looked under the front passenger seat.

"We have something," Owens shouted. Owens was holding a plastic wrapped block of whitish material.

Owens brought the bag to Barclay for him to examine. Being

careful not to open it, Barclay gave it a good sniff. He nodded to Owens. "Looks and smells like cocaine."

Carol was incredulous. "Cocaine. That's impossible. Then it dawned on her. It was planted by the MI6 agents. They likely also made the call to the Virginia State Police.

Carol and Tony had no recourse but to surrender to the troopers. Each was cuffed and rode separately in the cage-like back seat of the troopers' cars. They were taken to the Virginia State Police station in Lynchburg. Their BMW would later be towed to the same location.

A paunchy middle-aged trooper sat them down in a cramped windowless room and began to fill out a form.

"Let's see. The charge is possession of a pound of cocaine. Wow, that's worth a pretty penny." The trooper didn't look up when he spoke. "Hum, DC plates." He went on to take their names, ages, and used the address from their New York drivers' licenses. The New York connection prompted another, "Hum, New York address."

"I have all I need," concluded the desk-bound trooper. "Since you're married I'm putting you in the same cell." He led Carol and Tony to a standard cell with upper and lower bunk beds and an ancient toilet and sink in the corner. There was a small window on the back wall with bars higher than a normal person could reach.

"Unless you can make bail of $50,000, you'll be the guests of the Commonwealth of Virginia for now. You are allowed one phone call. Knock on the door if you want to make the call." With that the paunchy trooper locked the cell and left.

Carol and Tony both looked defeated. They didn't know what to do. They knew no one in Lynchburg.

Tony spoke first. "Should we call one of our parents? I know they'll believe us, but they could also gloat because they warned us not to leave. Or maybe we should call our friends in Raleigh? But, honestly, I don't know if our parents or our friends have the $50,000 for the bail."

Suddenly Carol looked hopeful. "We'll call neither our parents nor our friends. Instead, we'll call Walter Strom."

CHAPTER 30

Nogales, Mexico, Saturday, January 8, Early Morning

The President of Mexico controlled a highly skilled, secretive para-military unit called the Agentes de Aplicación Especial (Special Enforcement Operatives), or AAE for short. AAE was developed especially for combatting hardened criminals, like those in the drug cartels. With only fifty members, each agent was fluent in Spanish and English, had generalized skills in combat, surveillance, tracking, and capture, as well as a specialized skill in one of those four areas. The President could deploy AAE on his or her discretion, but each operation was later reviewed by a committee composed of members of the Mexican Congress. In recent years AAE had been tasked with apprehending drug cartel chiefs, rescuing victims of kidnappings, and investigating suspicious foreign activities.

Jorge immediately decided the taking of the mother of the Governor of Arizona was a job for AAE. Using Marie's mental map, he directed the leader of AAE, Colonel Jesus Sanchez, to move a detachment of AAE to Nogales, locate the kidnappers' hideout, and secure the release Maria. Although it was preferred the kidnappers be captured alive, Sanchez and AAE were permitted to inflict casualties. With the kidnappers' deadline ticking away, Sanchez had limited time to successfully complete the operation.

Sanchez had arrived in Nogales two days ago with twenty operatives. Maria's directions were so good that Sanchez was able to narrow down the location of the kidnappers to four blocks. He couldn't use helicopters to surveille the area for fear of spooking the kidnappers to flee. While that would put them out in the open and subject to his firepower, it would also significantly increase the chances Maria would not be recovered alive.

To pinpoint the exact house in the four block area, Sanchez first had several operatives pose as postal carriers, parcel deliverers, and utility workers. He had operatives trained in each of these tasks, and he also had arrangements with local governments and companies for his people to temporarily take the place of regular workers.

After a day of approaching every dwelling with mail or deliveries and many with utility work, Sanchez's second-in-command reported the results to him at the disguised mobile headquarters.

Sanchez looked up from studying a map as his colleague entered the Telmex van. "Remember, Diego, we're using English on this assignment, since the kidnappers are likely from the States."

"Yes sir," Diego replied. "Colonel Sanchez, based on the reconnaissance we've done, we think we have the house pinpointed." Diego pointed to an address on the map. "There's been no mail to the location, but we delivered a package, and although no one answered the door, the package was eventually taken in to the dwelling. Here's the photo of the person from our long-distance lens. The individual's name is Roberto Menendez, but his street name is Miquel. He works for Robert Fuentes and has a long arrest record. Menendez has also periodically left the dwelling in a black SUV and returned with bags, probably groceries. Here are the photos." Diego laid more long-distance photos on a table. "Based on the number of bags, we estimate there are six people in the dwelling. The SUV is parked in the driveway. We think there is another vehicle in the garage."

Diego produced a paper from his vest pocket. He unfolded it and spread it out on the table.

"Here's a map of the dwelling where we think Maria Vargas is being held, as well as the dwellings and terrain surrounding that house. There's a 35 degree decline in the back of the structure, but the ground on the other three sides is relatively flat."

Sanchez was pleased. "This is very good work, Diego. Now,

assuming you are correct, and Maria Vargas is being held by five others inside the dwelling, what tactics do you recommend? Remember, we have only four days left."

"First, I suggest one of our new silent drones lower both a camera and microphone through the chimney. The microphone is hyper-sensitive and will be able to detect noise throughout the house. Second, operatives can place our coin-sized fabric-penetrating cameras on each exterior window. Although we have had limited success with these cameras, in some operations they have provided us valuable information. Hopefully we can determine where Mrs. Vargas is located."

"These are all good suggestions. Go ahead and order them for tonight," commanded Sanchez. "Remember, although the drone can't be heard, it may be able to be seen, even at night. So, we still must surveille the dwelling for outside movement."

Diego nodded. "Yes, sir, we are constantly doing the outside surveillance."

"Good," agreed Sanchez.

Diego continued. "Last, and most important, six hours prior to the raid we'll order a high altitude infra-red scan of the dwelling. Such a scan was very helpful in the Monterrey operations in detecting any booby-traps and other electronic surprises. Then, if everything looks like a go, we'll drop gas canisters down the chimney and also shoot them inside when we break down the front door."

Sanchez leaned back in his chair and looked at the ceiling. He then rocked forward and stood up. "Diego, order the high altitude infra-red scan for tonight at 9 pm. Also, have our people program the drone to drop the camera and microphone down the chimney tonight, and have the specialized operatives place the fabric-penetrating cameras on the windows after dark. It's 7 am now. Schedule the break-in and rescue for 3 am tomorrow morning, 20 hours from now."

Maria spent most of her days watching television in the living room, often with Luis. She rarely saw Fuentes. He had a large well-furnished room – Maria had peeked – in the rear of the house. He seemed to be frequently talking on his cell phone. Miguel was in and out bringing groceries, food, and newspapers. Miguel let Maria cook occasionally, although under his watchful eyes, and Maria actually enjoyed his company. The other two men stayed mostly in the furnished basement, where there was another TV and some gym equipment. They even took their food downstairs.

Maria could tell Luis was troubled. She tried talking to him, but he would only mutter, "I made a big mistake, momma. I'm sorry. I'm no good," and then would disappear to his room.

Although Maria was not told, her sense and logic made her believe there was a deadline of some sort, and it was approaching. Earlier today while they were cooking together, Miguel had patted her on the back and said, "It won't be long now and you'll be back home." But Maria couldn't understand how they could let her go home since she'd seen their faces and knew some of their names. Only Maria's faith prevented her from screaming with fear.

Still, she wondered, how much longer?

CHAPTER 31

The Capitol, Washington, DC, Saturday, January 8, Early Morning

MARK WAS IN HIS OFFICE EARLY SATURDAY MORNING CATCHING UP on some Ag Committee reading. Denise had missed work on Friday. Mark didn't know if he was concerned, curious, or both. With his Ag reading quickly becoming boring, he decided to phone the number given for Denise on her personnel sheet. There was no answer. He did the same for Darlene – also with no success. He then noticed the numbers were the same. He thought of calling the Senate's human resource's office, but, of course, they were closed on Saturday.

Mark wondered if he should contact Lt. Evers. Since Denise was at least a 'persona of interest' in Bee Cooley's death, Evers likely wanted to keep trace of Denise's whereabouts.

Mark made the decision to call Evers.

"Lt. Evers, this is Senator Williams."

"Senator Williams, how coincidental of you to call." Evers always sounded very professional. "We think we may have the identity of a third person who was in Senator Cooley's apartment. We'd like to talk to Ms. Perdue and Ms. Huggins and see if they have any information about this person that could be helpful."

"That's what I was calling you about, Lieutenant. Ms. Perdue seems to be missing. And Ms. Huggins may be also."

There was a pause before Evers responded, "Interesting."

"Is there anything I can help with?" Mark thought he should at least offer.

"I don't think so, Senator. In fact, there's likely nothing I can do about Ms. Perdue and Ms. Huggins."

"Can't you put out your version of an APB – an all-points bulletin?"

"Yes, we could if it would help. But an APB only applies to our country."

"You mean Ms. Perdue and Ms. Huggins have left the country? Couldn't TSA have stopped them?" After he said this, Mark remembered how poorly funded TSA was.

"We don't think they left via flying. We think they were driven out of the country. Plus, even if we could have alerted our border agents, it probably wouldn't have mattered. We think Perdue and Huggins are foreign agents."

"They're what?"

"I said, we think they are foreign agents. Actually, they were foreign nationals working in the country with diplomatic immunity. But the nature of their work was espionage."

"If you don't mind me asking, how do you know, or surmise, this?"

"The FBI tries to keep track of foreign agents. Most of them just collect information and provide intelligence for their country. Ordinary stuff; nothing dramatic like we see in movies. I sent the prints and pictures of Perdue and Huggins to the FBI, and they confirmed the pair as foreign agents."

"For what country?"

"The UK. Perdue's real name is Pricilla Morton and Huggins is Daphne Basingstoke."

Now it made sense to Mark. There was always something not right about Denise's accent. He just couldn't place it as being from a region of South Carolina. Likely only a native like him could tell. And then, of course, was the complete switch in Denise's speech when Evers confronted her about her birth certificate.

"Lieutenant, this clears up a lot for me. Thanks. As foreign agents, could those two be capable of murder?"

"The FBI folks don't think so. Basingstoke and Morton would be more in to stealing information, planting false stories, and possibly blackmail. Certainly, all bad behavior, but nothing to the level of murder."

"You may not want to answer this question, Lieutenant Evers, but can you share the identity of the third set of the prints found in Senator Cooley's apartment?"

"Sure, I don't mind. I know you're new to the Senate, but if you run in to the person or hear information from other Senators, please contact me."

"Definitely, I will" Mark assured Evers.

"We found identifying information for Mr. Horace Cooley, Senator Cooley's ex-husband."

After completing the call with Evers, Mark let the avalanche of new information settle in his brain. Denise and Darlene – foreign agents – wow. Mark bet the British hustled them off to Canada, where they'd be untouchable. It was at least good Evers didn't think they were murderers.

Then there is Horace Cooley, perhaps the prime suspect in his former wife's murder. Aren't spouses at the top of the list for anyone's killing?

Mark's daydreaming of playing amateur detective was interrupted by the daily mail delivery. Dominating the stack was a manila envelope with his name and address hand-written. Mark opened it first. Inside was the same picture of Denise straddling him that he previously received. However, attached was a new note, which read, 'Nice job having your playmate removed. But we still have the goods on you. Remember, if you don't announce your support for Concon by tomorrow, this lovely picture will be every paper's front page story.'

Mark now saw the connection.

CHAPTER 32

Lynchburg, Virginia, Saturday, January 8, Mid Afternoon

Carol dialed Warren Strom's number. 'Please answer, please answer,' she said quietly to herself.

The ringing stopped. "Strom here."

"Mr. Strom, this is Carol Shipman. My husband Tony and I are big fans. We are in Lynchburg and have some information we're sure you will find very, very interesting that only you can deliver to the country." Carol knew her initial statement to Strom was crucial to attracting his attention.

"You do, Ms. Shipman." Carol thought Strom sounded skeptical, but at least he hadn't hung up. "What is the nature of this information?"

Carol thought – don't rush, but be concise. "Mr. Strom, I worked for the British Embassy in Washington. Among other things I did press releases. You may have seen the press release I did about a *Le Monde* article on a new Franco-Spanish alliance."

Strom interrupted. "Yes, I did see that. Highly entertaining, although not believable."

"Well, I mistakenly received an official British government document outlining a plan to take advantage of our country's political divisions in order to establish a new British Empire in the world."

Carol paused to let Strom reply. He didn't. "Mr. Strom, did you hear what I said?"

"I did. Please continue."

"Sir, the document details how the British are working to see that Concon – the call for a new Constitutional Convention…"

"I know what Concon is, Ms. Shipman."

"Excuse me, Mr. Strom, of course you do. Anyway, the document talks about British agents spreading false information and engaging in blackmail in order to get Concon authorized. They expect Concon to result in a much-weakened federal government – maybe something like the Articles of Confederation – that will allow states to essentially become free agents. Then the British can pick off and absorb the ones they want into their new Empire."

"Free agents – I like your sports analogy."

Carol was worried Strom wasn't taking her seriously. "Mr. Strom, if this happens, it's the end of our country."

"Some say our country is already gone."

"Well, I don't, and neither does my husband. In fact, we know many people who want to keep the country together and strong." As soon as she said the words, Carol was afraid Strom might be one of the doubters."

"Ms. Shipman, I like your passion. You're obviously a smart person. Let's say all of what you say is true. Why did you come to me? What can I do?"

"Mr. Strom, my mother and father listened to you when you were on the networks. Tony and I still listen to you. We think you're about the only person with enough credibility and respect to convince the country about the seriousness of this plot. The country needs you to save it from itself." There it was, Carol mused. This was the best she could do.

"Ms. Shipman, you flatter me, which is not a bad thing as long as it's sincere. I believe you are sincere. You said you were in Lynchburg. Can you bring this document to my home and let me study it?"

"Thank you, thank you, Mr. Strom. We certainly do want to show it to you. But there's one problem."

"There is?" Strom now sounded uneasy.

"I know this will sound far-fetched, but what I am going to tell you is absolutely the truth. When the British Embassy found the document missing and decided I had it, they sent agents chasing us."

"Chasing you where? To Lynchburg?"

"We had already decided to come to Lynchburg to see you. But yes, they were chasing us on our drive here. When we stayed overnight at a motel at Manassas, the agents broke into our room, drugged us, and stole –what they thought – was the real report. Fortunately, we had hidden the real report in our car. Then the agents must have placed some cocaine in our car and then called the state police. The police stopped us, found the cocaine – which is absolutely not ours – and now we are in the Virginia State Police station in downtown Lynchburg. We were hoping you could help get us released. Then we can look at the report."

"Now I see the picture. You're a couple of coke head drug runners who want to scam me into getting you released."

Carol's heart sank. "Oh, no, no, no Mr. Strom. Everything I've told you is absolutely true. I'm not a drug dealer. I have a Ph.D. in European history. You have to believe me," sniffled Carol.

Strom could tell Carol was crying. Although Strom had a stern exterior, he had a soft interior, and sobbing females were one of his weaknesses. He remembered Carol's name being associated with the *Le Monde* press release, so at least that much was true. He was also intrigued by the idea of a new British Empire. Strom decided to take a chance.

"Ms. Shipman, here's what I'll offer you. Since you're a history expert, I'll administer a little test. There will be three questions – the answers are dates in years. You answer all three correctly and I'll come to the station and help free you and your husband. Get any of the three wrong and I'll hang up. And, I'll also report this attempted scam to the police, which will likely make the case against you stronger. You see, I am a well-liked celebrity around here. So, do you want to take the test?"

Carol composed herself and didn't hesitate. "Yes"

"When was the Magna Carta signed?"

"1215."

"When was U.S. Constitution *ratified*?"

Carol noticed Strom's emphasis on 'ratified' rather than 'effective'. "1788."

"Last, when was the U.S. Civil War – or, as some call it, the War between the States - concluded?

"1865."

"Ms. Shipman. It would be a highly unusual drug dealer who could answer all three of those questions correctly. You did. So, I will help secure the release of you and your husband. Then we'll take a good look at this British plot to steal our country. Also, if you are lying and are a drug dealer, I still want to meet you, because you would be unique, and I like unique people. There's one more thing, Ms. Shipman. You are obviously a person with some level of higher education. I'll ask you one more question. It's free – you already have earned your get-out-of-jail card - but I'm curious if you know the answer. The question is, what is the significance of those three questions?"

Carol felt like she was back in graduate school, but it was a good feeling. She was confident she knew the answer.

"Mr. Strom, those are the three most important events in the development of the United States' political system."

"Ms. Shipman, I'll see you within the hour. And, well-done."

Walter Strom strode into the Virginia State Police station forty minutes later. He was a distinguished looking man who carried himself with confidence. A shy under 6-foot, medium build but with the sagging frame characteristic of a plus 70-year old, Strom wore a business grey three-piece suit with a bright gold tie and matching gold cufflinks. Most noticeable was a full head of yellowish-grey hair parted exactly in the middle and then with each half combed to the side. Strom was accompanied by a less-distinguished individual in his mid-forties, balding, glasses, and wearing a mis-matched rumpled brown jacket with darker brown slacks.

The paunchy desk trooper jumped up upon seeing Strom enter.

"Mr. Strom, what a pleasure. What brings you here?"

"I've come with my attorney, Cletus Humphrey, to see some acquaintances of mine, Carol and Tony Shipman. I believe they are staying at your distinguished facility."

The trooper looked surprised. "We just brought them in today. Cocaine found in their vehicle. You know them?"

"Yes I do," Strom said firmly. "They are business associates. They tell me the cocaine was planted by foreign agents. I believe them. Mr. Humphrey and I would like to see them."

Still perplexed, the officer nevertheless agreed and showed Strom and Humphrey to Carol and Tony's cell. The cell was unlocked by the officer, and Strom and Humphrey entered.

"I can bring some chairs, Mr. Strom," offered the officer.

"That won't be necessary, officer. We won't be long."

"I'm sorry Mr. Strom, but regulations require I lock you in. Just yell when you're ready to leave."

"I will. Thank you, officer."

Carol and Tony looked relieved. Carol wanted to hug Strom, but noticing his formal dress and manner, she didn't think he was the hugging type. She introduced Tony to Strom and Humphrey.

"Mr. Strom, Tony and I can't thank you enough for coming and believing in us."

Strom smiled, but was all business. "First, we need to get you released. This is what Mr. Humphrey is for. Then I need to see the British report you have." Strom turned to look at Humphrey.

Humphrey took over. "We have an excellent case for your release and maybe even complete dismissal of the case. First, your car was unattended last evening. I have documentation of your stay at the Comfort Inn." He pulled out a sheet from his briefcase showing the reservation and payment. "Your vehicle was vulnerable to entry and the planting of the cocaine. Second, I checked summons, arrest and incarnation records for both of you in New York. There's nothing, not even a traffic ticket. In legal language, you have no priors. Third, and perhaps most important, Mr. Strom will vouch for your character and reason for being in the area. He will state that, due to the sensitive nature of your work, there are interests that would benefit from your arrests. Now, if you will excuse me, I will make a phone call to a judge and see if we can wrap this up in quick order."

Carol and Tony could only look spellbound at Humphrey as he moved to a corner of the cell and dialed a number from his phone. Strom put his finger to his mouth to indicate no talking while Humphrey conducted business. Humphrey was talking away from the trio, so nothing was clearly heard.

After only a few minutes, Humphrey ended the conversation and returned to the group. "That was straightforward. Mr. and Mrs. Shipman are to be released in the custody of Mr. Strom. Judge Early will have to verify their information – which I will forward to him when I return to my office – but if it's all in order, the case will likely be dropped."

"So are we're free to go now?" asked a flabbergasted Tony.

"Yes," acknowledged Humphrey, "but as I said, in the custody of Mr. Strom. The officer on duty should be appearing any minute after receiving a call from Judge Early ordering your release."

Just as Humphrey predicted, the chubby desk trooper appeared and unlocked the cell door.

"You're being released in the custody of Mr. Strom," he said, looking at Carol and Tony. "Also, here are the keys to your car, which is parked in our lot out back. Every 24 hours you are to report your location to this station, with verification from Mr. Strom, while the case is still pending. Understand?"

"Yes, sir, we do," Tony answered as he took the car keys.

Humphrey whispered to Carol and Tony, "It won't be pending long."

Strom, Humphrey, Carol, and Tony excited the station and walked to the parking lot.

"You have the report hidden somewhere in your car?" inquired Strom. "That was brilliant to have planted a phony duplicate in your luggage."

"That was Carol's idea, Mr. Strom. But it was my idea where to hide the real report on the car."

Strom stopped and surveyed the BMW. After a few minutes he uttered, “Rocker panels.”

“I can’t believe it, you’re right, Mr. Strom,” explained Tony. “How did you know?”

“Best hiding place in the world. *The French Connection* taught us that. Now, let’s head to my home and develop a plan to end the next British Empire before it even begins.”

CHAPTER 33

Lynchburg, Virginia, Saturday, January 8, Late Afternoon

Warren Strom lived in an antebellum three-story home high on a hill overlooking the James River in downtown Lynchburg. His wife had passed five years ago. He rambled about the ten-room home all alone except for a live-in cook and housekeeper.

Yet it was more than Strom's home. It was also his office. Half of the first floor was a fully functioning radio station. Strom had state-of-the-art equipment for both live broadcasts and recordings. There was a commercial grade thirty-foot antenna in the backyard that enabled direct satellite connections. From the satellites Strom could reach every broadcasting station – both radio and TV – in the country, and his broadcasts could be streamed to all internet providers. Strom could also connect to stations in Mexico, Canada, and parts of the Caribbean. His programs could be streamed anywhere in the world.

In addition, the second floor of the home was a radio museum. Classic radios from as far back as the twenties were neatly arranged on walnut bookcases. Walls were adorned with posters of important individuals in radio history, including Marconi, Murrow, Cronkite, and Godfrey. There were even a couple posters of the 'shock jocks', Howard Stern and Don Imus. Then, of course, were pictures of

Strom throughout the decades on his climb to fame as the most trusted voice in broadcasting of the last fifty years.

Strom, Carol, and Tony entered the house and settled in the historically decorated parlor to the left of the main entrance. A middle-aged woman with pulled-back brown-grey hair and wearing an apron suddenly appeared.

"Mr. Strom, should I serve refreshments?

A stickler for manners, Strom first made introductions.

"Madilyn, this is Carol and Tony Shipman. They're originally from New York, and they've had quite an ordeal. I think they are going to be a great help to me, and to the country. And Carol and Tony, this lovely woman is Madilyn Worster, my right-hand person who handles my housekeeping, schedule, and overall management of yours-truly, all tasks that my late wife used to do." Strom abruptly stopped, apparently fighting back some tears at the thought of his departed mate. "Madilyn is also a superb cook."

Carol and Tony rose, crossed the room and shook hands with Madilyn while expressing pleasure at meeting her.

Now composed, Strom offered a plan. "Both of you must be tired and perhaps want to freshen up," he said looking at Carol and Tony. "I suggest Madilyn show you to the upstairs guest room and bathroom. The bathroom has both a shower and bathtub, so use whichever you prefer. I have a contact in England who is a retired MI6 agent. With your permission, I'd like to scan the report and then email it to him. After you have relaxed, we can discuss the report over dinner. So, maybe reconvene in two hours?"

"That sounds like a great plan, Mr. Strom," answered Carol. I have to admit Tony and I are a little tired, and we probably do need to clean up too."

Madilyn motioned them to the hallway stairs.

"Oh, by the way Madilyn, what are you serving for dinner tonight?" asked Strom.

"It's Italian night, Mr. Strom. I made vegetarian lasagna with a tomato and spinach salad. And there's homemade lemon meringue pie for dessert. I hope that pleases everyone."

"It certainly does us. We can't wait. Our stomachs are a little empty," answered Tony.

Precisely two hours later Carol and Tony walked into the dining room. They both had showered and put on fresh clothes, although they were wrinkled from the MI6 agents tossing them around. Strom was already seated at the table holding a glass of red wine and looking at the report.

Ever the gentleman, he rose upon seeing Carol and motioned the couple to seats near his. Although not experts, Carol and Tony guessed the pieces of furniture in the room were antiques, probably from the 19th century. Wallpaper depicting wildflowers dominated by pale pink and green colors covered the walls. A large chandelier, also likely an antique, illuminated the room.

"Care for a glass of pinot noir?" asked Strom. "I like red wine with Italian food, and pinot noir is my favorite red. Of course, it you'd rather have white, I can offer that for you also."

Carol and Tony agreed the pinot noir would be just fine, and they watched Strom give them generous glassfuls.

"My ex-MI6 friend has already responded. First, and most importantly, he confirmed the report is real. Now, let me quickly say, I believed both of you, but if I am about to make a worldwide broadcast claiming there is a British plot to encourage the dismemberment of the United States, then I need confirmation that allegation is true."

"Mr. Strom, we certainly understand and agree," responded Carol. "Even I had my doubts the report was genuine."

The discussion paused as Madilyn served Strom and his guests the salads. Strom also replenished everyone's wine glasses.

"Madilyn, this salad is delectable," announced Tony after taking a bite. Carol also added her 'thumbs up.'

"Madilyn is an outstanding cook. She has never served me a bad meal," commented Strom. Madilyn beamed.

After finishing his salad, Strom continued. "My contact also said the report is consistent with noise he and friends have heard about a plan to reassemble parts of the British Empire. Sort of like the band getting back together." Strom chuckled at his analogy. "However, this is the first time he's seen anything in print."

"I wonder why the British took the chance of putting the plan on paper" asked Tony. "Surely they realized there was a possibility the report could somehow be leaked to the public."

Strom was impressed. "Good point, Tony. My answer is, the bureaucracy. This plan is being carried out by more than the MI6 folks. It also involves several bureaus, agencies, and departments in the British government. And anytime the bureaucracy is involved, so is turf. Bureaucracies are constantly competing over position and power, which are other names for influence. As a result, bureaucracies have to see plans on paper so they can argue and negotiate among themselves."

"Mr. Strom is absolutely right,' added Carol. "Did you know bureaucratic infighting during World War II almost made D-Day a disaster?"

Smiling at Carol's comment, Strom pushed his clean salad plate aside. "I also think there's a likelihood the British carefully guarded the report, but someone purposefully provided it to Carol. In other words, someone on the inside of the British Embassy didn't like the second empire idea and wanted to sabotage it."

Strom and Tony both looked at Carol, who was now considering the possibility of an inside leaker. Could it have been someone from the media room?

Salads done, Madilyn now served the main course of vegetarian lasagna. Carol and Tony had never had this dish before, yet they avidly dug in.

"Oh, my, this is out of this world. Madilyn, you should be in a five-star restaurant," exclaimed Carol. "Can I get the recipe?"

Madilyn smiled broadly. "Of course. I'm glad you like it."

"Now wait a minute, Madilyn. I don't want you leaving me for some high-end eatery," teased Strom.

"Never, Mr. Strom. Never."

The group was quiet while each savored the lasagna. When he was almost done, Strom rested his fork and spoke.

"The country needs to know about this plot. Tomorrow I will begin preparing a broadcast, which I plan to give next Wednesday. I already have my people promoting it, and I've contacted my supporters to ask for more resources so we can put out the word even more widely. I hope you can stay until then and watch the broadcast live."

"We'd be honored to, Mr. Strom. Thank you for including us, and thank you for informing the country," Carol said for both her and Tony.

"There is one other item my MI6 contact shared that is disturbing, if not dangerous."

Carol and Tony's mood turned to worry. "What is it, Mr. Strom," asked Tony.

"He said there are two categories of backers for Concon. The first he describes as 'soft backers,' meaning they will use personal intimidation, the media, and even blackmail to promote their cause, but never physical violence. The second group he labels 'hard backers.' They will use any means, including murder."

Carol and Tony dropped their forks.

CHAPTER 34

Nogales, Mexico, Sunday, January 9, Early Morning

Sanchez looked at his watch. It was 2:45 am. Everything was in place for the raid on the kidnappers' dwelling. A camera and microphone had been lowered into the structure through the chimney. Fabric piercing remote cameras had secretly been placed on all windows. The aerial infra-red scan revealed no electronic traps. All indications suggested everyone was asleep.

The canister thrown into the house would disable, but not harm, the occupants. Agents wearing oxygen masks would swam into the dwelling and quickly apprehend the kidnappers before any could resist.

"Diego, is the gas canister ready and all agents positioned for entry?"

"Yes sir, everything is ready. I am in contact with the field commander. At your order, I will tell her to begin the operation."

"Excellent." Sanchez took another sip of green tea. It calmed him. Sanchez always worried before starting an operation. Although meticulous planning had occurred and all contingencies considered, there was always the possibility something had been overlooked or simply not known. He remembered a raid on drug dealers in Cancun. They were in a suite on the eighth floor of a ten-story hotel. Each member of the team kept a small gas mask in their pocket. The mask was capable of providing oxygen for only ten minutes. But that was enough time for the dealers to hold off Sanchez's agents while they repelled down the side of the building to waiting vehicles. Three of Sanchez's agents were killed and four wounded.

It was exactly 3 am. "Diego, commence the operation."

Diego spoke into his smart wrist watch to the field commander. "Begin the operation."

Sanchez and Diego left the command post for the kidnappers' dwelling just a block away. They immediately heard a loud 'boom' as the gas canister was propelled through the demolished front doorway. Fifteen heavily armed AAE agents followed.

Gas masks on and pistols drawn, Sanchez and Diego hurried to the front porch. They would stay out of the way and let the well-trained agents do their work. Sanchez was anxious to see Maria Vargas brought out unharmed.

If the operation went according to plan, there would be no gunshots. Unfortunately, this was not to be the case. Within seconds after arriving, Sanchez heard rapid shots from several automated weapons. What could have gone wrong, he worried.

What Sanchez and AAE missed was the basement. The plans of the house on file with the Nogales city government showed no basement. Within seconds of hearing the front door battered in and before the gas could penetrate the rear bedrooms, Miguel and the two guards herded Maria and Luis into the basement where automatic weapons and ammunition were stored. Fuentes was not in the house.

As AAE agents cautiously peered down the basement stairs, bursts of fire shot past them.

"One more step and the old woman is dead," screamed Miguel from the basement.

The agents backed off and the situation was relayed to Sanchez. He and Diego immediately entered the house and proceeded to the basement stairs in the rear. They were met by the operations commander, Juanita Martinez.

"What's the status?" barked Sanchez.

"Sir, we were unaware of the basement. It appears the hostage and kidnappers are there, and the kidnappers are heavily armed."

Sanchez approached the top of the stairs. "Who am I talking to?" he yelled into the stairwell.

"You can call me Miguel, Colonel Sanchez. I know who you are and you probably know who I am."

Sanchez wasn't surprised. Someone in Miguel's occupation was surely aware of AAE.

"Release the hostage, throw down your weapons, and no one will be harmed" ordered Sanchez. "You have no way to escape." Sanchez knew his offer would be rejected.

"I know you have to try, Colonel, but there's no way that's going to happen. Instead, here is what will occur. You and your colleagues will leave the house and return to your command post. My guess is it's a block or two away. I'll then lead my little party out of the house to our nice SUV in the driveway, and then we're off. And one more thing. Don't put any fancy tracking devices on the SUV. If I find any, that will shorten the life of the lovely Mrs. Vargas. And I'd hate to do that. I've so enjoyed cooking with her."

Sanchez had no choice. "Agreed. We're leaving now."

Sanchez, Diego, Martinez, and the other AAE agents reluctantly left the house for the command trailer. Fortunately, no agent had been harmed, but clearly the pride and reputation of Sanchez had. Sanchez knew the President would not be happy, and he might even ask for Sanchez's resignation.

At the command trailer, the AAE agents still kept watch on the front porch. Ten minutes elapsed with no sign of the kidnappers or Maria Vargas. Then twenty minutes, then half an hour, then forty-five minutes. Sanchez was worried.

"Diego, is the microphone we inserted into the chimney still working?"

"Yes, sir."

"Have we heard any movement?"

"No sir."

Odd, thought Sanchez.

"Diego, you, Martinez, and two agents go back to the house. Be cautious and quiet. If you can, go inside and see what's happening."

"Yes, sir, right away."

Minutes which seemed like hours elapsed. Finally, Sanchez's wrist phone buzzed.

"Give me a report Diego. What have you found?"

"Colonel, you won't believe this. No one was on the main floor. We went into the basement and found everyone gone except one person. Ms. Vargas was there, gagged and bound, but fine as far as we can determine. It looks as though the rest escaped through a tunnel."

"Tunnel," shouted Sanchez. First, he missed the basement and now a tunnel that provided an easy exit. Sanchez was a detail person – you had to be in his profession - and he was angry he had missed two critical details. Still, at the same time he was relieved. He had accomplished the mission of securing the release of Maria Vargas. But any serious observer would conclude it wasn't the result of his efforts; it was in spite of his efforts.

Where did the kidnappers go? And why did the kidnappers give up Maria Vargas so easily?

Sanchez was sure of one thing. The President of Mexico, his boss, would have the same questions.

CHAPTER 35

Phoenix, Arizona, Sunday, January 9, Late Morning

THERESA WAS IN ST RAPHAEL'S CHURCH WITH FLORES, NICK, AND Sophia. Every time a prayer was said, she said it in honor of Maria. Nick had told her about his meeting with Jorge, but neither he nor Theresa had received any updates. The more days that went by without Maria, the more worried Theresa became.

One of the downsides of being Governor was the need to be in constant communication with staff in case of an emergency. Every time Theresa's cell phone rang or buzzed at an unlikely time, she knew the news was likely not good. Hence, when Theresa's cell vibrated in the middle of the service, she immediately felt knots form in her stomach.

Theresa looked at the caller ID. It was Emily. Theresa discreetly rose from the pew and walked to an adjoining room.

"Yes, Emily. Is it about my mother?" Theresa anxiously answered.

"Governor, the President of Mexico, Jorge Guerrero, is on the line."

Theresa took a deep breath, made the sign of the cross, and spoke into the phone.

"Mr. President, what a delight it is to talk to you," Theresa nervously began.

"As it is for me, Madame Governor. And let me quickly apologize for contacting you on our holy day, but what I have to tell you is very important."

Theresa tensely awaited Guerrero's next statement.

"Governor Vargas. I have some very good news for you. We have rescued your mother, Maria."

It took all of Theresa's strength to not throw now the phone, jump for joy, and let out a jubilant scream. Then emotion overtook her and the tears started to flow.

"God ... God bless you, Mr. President," Theresa stammered. "Thank you. Gracias."

Even over the phone Guerrero could sense Theresa's emotion, and it affected him as he wiped away a tear. "You know, in our culture mothers are considered saints. You will soon have your Saint Maria back. My security people are taking her right now to the border, where she will be turned over to your state police. And by the way, please call me Jorge."

"Thank you, Jorge. I can't wait to see my mother and hug her. And call me Theresa. I would love to host you and your wife for a visit and offer my gratitude in person."

"That would be most wonderful, Theresa. As they say, I will have my people contact your people to work out the details."

Theresa now turned serious. "Jorge, can you tell me anything about the kidnappers and the rescue?"

"Here's what we know. Robert Fuentes appears to have been the leader, although my people don't think he actually participated in apprehending your mother. There were four others in the group, one – named Roberto Menendez – is a well-known criminal with links to the drug cartel. Unfortunately, all escaped. There was a tunnel from the house that we weren't aware of."

"Does this mean they could have taken my mother with them?"

"It appears so. She was in the basement bound and gagged near the exit to the tunnel. We're certainly glad your mother was left behind, but my people are trying to determine the reason."

"Whatever the reason, I'm glad. I have one more question, Jorge. Was my brother Luis Vargas one of the kidnappers?" Theresa braced herself for the answer.

"I honestly can't say, Theresa. Other than Fuentes and Menendez, we don't have the names of the other kidnappers. However, we do have some photos of them taken from high-tech cameras we placed on the windows. When the photos are processed, I'll have copies sent to you."

"Thank you. Jorge, you've been most gracious and helpful. I'll be forever indebted to you and your team for saving my mother. I look forward to seeing you and your wife here in Arizona. Good bye for now."

"You are welcome. Amila and I greatly anticipate visiting you and your great state. And by the way. That system your mother and you devised for communicating directions worked wonderfully. We may want to hire Maria to teach it to our agents. Adios Governor Theresa."

The homecoming on Monday for Maria was an event. The City of Phoenix closed a four-street section to accommodate the thousands of supporters and well-wishers. Theresa, Flores, Alexandro, Sophia, and Nick waited on Maria's porch as a multi-car caravan carried Maria up and down streets in the neighborhood. Even though temperatures barely reached the 60s, Maria sat in the backseat of a friend's 1960s Cadillac convertible with the top down and waved like either a politician or beauty queen. Today, she could have been both. Theresa was sure that if Maria were running for mayor, she'd be elected in a landslide. She could possibly even had won Theresa's job.

The procession ended at Maria's home. Loud cheers erupted as Maria left the convertible for her porch. There were long embraces from each of her family, with chants of 'speech, speech' in the background.

Indeed, a microphone had been set up on the porch, complete with the Arizona State Seal attached. Theresa stepped up to it first.

"I know you want to hear from our returning friend, my mother, Maria Vargas." Theresa pointed to her beaming mother as cheers again erupted. "So I won't speak very long. I just want to say, first as a daughter and second as Governor, how blessed we are that you were brought back to us safely." Theresa looked at Maria as she said the words and noticed Maria's face was covered with tears. "I also want to thank the great nation of Mexico, and especially its President, Jorge Guerrero, for undertaking the effort that brought Maria back to us." There were again cheers but this time mixed with a few boos. "Now, here she is, my mother and your friend and neighbor, Maria Vargas." As Theresa switched places with Maria, a face in the crowd caught her eye.

The crowd went wild. There was thunderous applause and cries of 'Maria, Maria.' Theresa and Maria kissed each other's cheeks, and Theresa sat down as Maria basked in the adulation. She really should run for something, thought Theresa.

Surprising her daughter, Maria removed a piece of paper from her pocket. The note contained names of people Maria wanted to thank, and it was a long list. Included were the names of several Arizona State Police officers, numerous agents of the Mexican AAE Maria had met, including Sanchez and Diaz, the President of Mexico, and Phoenix public works employees and city police who managed the parade and celebration. She also thanked her son Luis, who she said helped her get through the kidnapping ordeal.

Maria ended her 'thank you' with a large wave and a two-handed blowing of kisses. Theresa's security detail began to usher the Governor to her SUV but she waved them off. Instead, Theresa followed Maria into the kitchen with the security detail rushing to catch up.

"They did a great job on repairing the door," Maria concluded as she looked the door up and down and back and forth.

"Yes, they did," Theresa agreed without looking. "Momma, I need to ask you something. You thanked Luis for helping you survive the kidnapping. Was Luis there with you?"

Maria smiled. "Yes he was. I don't know what I would have done without him. Miguel was also kind to me. We cooked together. But it was good to have a blood relative close by."

"Was Luis also kidnapped?"

"I don't think so. He was there when they brought me to the

house. He didn't seem to spend a lot of time with the others. He mostly watched television all day and night."

"Did you see him leave through the tunnel?"

"Oh, Tessa, everything happened so fast. It was all a blur. Someone – I think Miguel – picked me up, carried me to the basement, and then tied and gagged me. Everyone else was gone."

Theresa gave Maria a kiss on her forehead. "Now, Momma, remember some workmen are coming by to install a security system for your home. I know you'll offer them some food. That's fine, but please don't bother them too much. They have other jobs after yours."

"I promise to be good, Tessa," Marie responded with a sly smile.

"And I almost forgot. They'll be a state trooper posted outside your home from 7 pm to 7 am. Also, please don't bother her or him."

"Not even for some coffee and cookies?"

"OK, coffee and cookies are fine, but that's it."

After another kiss and hug Theresa was off to her office with the security detail. The streets were quiet now and the barricades were being removed. Then it came to her. Theresa's subconscious must have been working during the conversation with Maria. That face in the crowd. It was Luis.

CHAPTER 36

The Capitol, Washington, DC. Monday, January 10, Early Morning

MARK BRACED HIMSELF AS HE LOOKED AT THE FRONT PAGE OF THE *Washington Reporter.* He had missed the photo-blackmailer's demand of a show of support for Concon by Sunday to prevent the compromising picture of him and Denise from being released to the press. Mark had never had any intention of meeting the demand, and today would reveal if the threat was true.

It was. The picture of Denise and him in the pose that clearly suggested more than the typical senator-secretary relationship took almost half of the front page. Mark's mind immediately raced back to the famous photo of the powerful Congressman Wilber Mills cavorting with the stripper Fannie Foxe in the tidal basin near the Jefferson Memorial. Mills was the chairman of the House Ways and Means Committee, which meant Mills controlled all tax legislation moving through the Congress. In the 1960s and early 1970s, few people were more influential as Mills. That influence ended with a splash in the wee hours of an October morning in 1974.

Mark certainly didn't have the power of Mills, but he did have a personal life which mattered most to him. He could take the political heat. He couldn't take losing his marriage and family. He hoped he could explain the picture to Cheryl.

Mark's next phone call would dash that hope. Mark heard the buzz of his private cell line. It was Cheryl.

Mark knew the call was about the photo, which likely also made the South Carolina papers, so he got right to the point. "Hello, Cheryl. I suppose you're calling about the photo."

Cheryl was direct. "I sure am. My next call is to a divorce attorney. I know he'll ask if there is some explanation, so just to expedite things, I thought I'd listen to any lame excuse you have."

"I know you won't believe me, and I know you'll do what you want. But I am innocent. Denise – and that's not her real name; I'll explain later – came on to me. I did absolutely nothing to encourage her, and the photo you see is as far as things went. I made it clear to Denise that we only had a professional relationship."

"That's what you say." Mark could hear the venom in her voice. "But just because it entertains me, you said Denise is someone else. Who is she, a hooker you paid for?"

"Of course not. She is – or was – a British agent meant to spy on me and, quite frankly, paid to blackmail me over my vote on Concon."

"Really. Well, talk about a far-fetched story. I guess if you're going to lie, you may as well make it interesting."

"I'm telling the truth, Cheryl. You can check with Lt. Evers of the DC Police. He tried to arrest her."

"So why didn't he? Was he getting a couple of tricks too?"

"No, the British whisked Denise and her accomplice Darlene out of the country before Evers could apprehend them."

"Denise and Darlene – cute – sort of like twins. Is it more fun with twins?"

"Look, Cheryl, I know you're mad. But I only love you and the boys. I'm telling you the total truth. Please think about it and give me a chance before you go to the attorney."

"Oh, you'll have your chance alright – in court." The call ended.

Mark knew talking to Cheryl would be difficult, but not this difficult. He'd give her a few days to cool down and then try again. Maybe he could get Evers to help about the twins.

Mark hadn't yet received a replacement for Denise – Pricilla – so he was all alone in the office. He had reports from the Ag Committee to read, so he spent several hours plowing through topics like price supports, countervailing tariffs, and climate change contributing to animal stress. A couple of nabs – cheese crackers with peanut butter between them – and a Pepsi from the vending machine sufficed for lunch.

Halfway through the afternoon Mark needed a break, so he decided to visit his colleague Joe Ferguson. Joe was a good listener, so Mark could unburden himself a little. Mark also wanted to see if Joe had heard anymore from his blackmailers. If Mark's exposure was used as an example, other Senators would probably be reminded to vote for Concon or they'd be next.

Bee Cooley's office was on the way to Ferguson's. When Mark passed it the door was closed, but he could hear shouting. He opened the door to see what was happening.

"Don't you dare tell me I can't see my wife's files. Who in the hell do you think you are?" A large Black man, well over six feet tall, with a narrow waist, broad shoulders, and muscular arms, was glaring at the secretary who had replaced Darlene.

"But, sir, you are Senator Cooley's ex-husband. And the DC Police have clearly told us not to allow anyone see the Senator's files while the murder investigation is on-going."

"You do have the keys, don't you, you little shit? Give them to me before I twist you into a pretzel."

"Hey, hey, what's going on here? Mark moved to take a position between the secretary and the Black man. "You have no right to threaten a federal employee. What's your problem?"

"Who in the hell are you?" snorted the angry man.

"I'm Senator Mark Williams. I was a colleague of Bee Cooley. The young lady is correct. There is still a murder investigation going on, and nothing leaves this office without the permission of the DC Police."

"I don't care what you or the DC Police say. I'm Horace Cooley, Bee's husband. Husbands have legal rights to their wife's belongings."

Mark held his ground. The secretary had taken cover behind her desk. "Actually, you don't since you're the ex-husband. So why don't you cool down and quietly leave." Mark emphasized his statement by pointing to the door.

Horace didn't budge. "Wait a minute, I know you. I saw you and two women rummaging around Bee's office one night. I bet you have the codes."

Mark was confused. "Codes, what codes?"

"The codes to her bank accounts so I can get my money. I saw you take some papers from here. They were the codes, weren't they? Give them to me." Horace moved toward Mark.

Mark retreated a few feet with the palms of his hands held in front of him, all the while wondering if Horace was the person who knocked him out the same night he was in Bee's office with Denise and Darlene.

"Slow down, Horace. Let's talk about this. You're angry now. Let's go get a cup of coffee and talk."

Meanwhile, oblivious to Horace, the secretary was carefully dialing for security.

Mark was now backed up to the secretary's desk with nowhere to go.

Horace lunged at Mark. "I don't want to talk, I want my money, and you're going to give it to me."

That was the last thing Mark heard before he felt a direct punch to his chin.

CHAPTER 37

Phoenix, Arizona, Tuesday, January 11, Early Morning

ROBERT FUENTES WAS BITTER. THE KIDNAPPING OF THE GOVERNOR'S mother was foiled. Those providing him with financial backing abruptly ordered him to abort the operation as soon as the AAE showed up. He didn't understand why. He held all the cards. He was certain the Governor would cave and support Concon if it meant saving her mother's life. But he wasn't given enough time to find out. To make matters worse, his backers also cancelled the funding of the Concon ads, just when it appeared they were having an impact on public sentiment.

Fuentes wasn't a person to quit. He didn't stop fighting his competitors in business, even though his success was much smaller than his lifestyle projected. He was lucky to have powerful and rich friends.

Fuentes had enough money for one last operation. He still seethed at Theresa Vargas, whom he considered to be the major roadblock to his dream of a revived Mexican Empire. Fuentes pictured himself as the Emperor of that empire.

A U.S. governor hadn't been assassinated since 1900. Fuentes aimed to change that. Powerful people are always vulnerable when they travel. Their homes and offices can be fortified and protected with technology and scores of guards. Once on the move they leave that protection and are subject to circumstances not under their control.

On most days Theresa's security detail drove her from the bungalow to the Governor's office at 7:30 am. The route is periodically changed and is unknown to the public. However, one of Fuentes' men had gained access to the route schedule on a recent visit to the Governor's home. That man was Luis.

The plan was simple. Approximately half-way through Theresa's twenty-minute ride to the office, her state SUV would slow to make a sharp right-hand turn. With most downtown businesses and offices not opening until 9 or 10, the streets would be largely empty. After turning, Theresa's SUV would be blocked by a car driven by Miguel and including one of Fuentes' guards. A second car, with Fuentes, the other guard, and Luis, would come up behind Theresa's SUV. Theresa's SUV would be hit with withering AK-47 shots from both ahead and behind. Even the vehicle's bullet-proof glass would not be able to withstand the firepower. Fuentes would have his revenge.

Theresa was anxious to get to the office. She had a lot on her mind – the aftermath of Maria's kidnapping, her speech to the opening of the legislature later in the week, and the knowledge Luis was apparently working with Maria's abductor, Fuentes.

It was unlike Theresa to run late. Flores was taken to school by a separate security detail. But Flores had a presentation to give today, and she wanted to make one last trial run in front of Theresa. Theresa never wanted to be a parent who discouraged her child's learning, and she also wanted – whenever she could – to put her family ahead of work. Theresa therefore agreed to listen once again to Flores' fifteen-minute presentation.

Rather than leaving the bungalow at 7:30, Theresa and the security detail didn't get started until 7:45. Theresa sat in the back seat behind the driver. A guard sat on her right. Sgt. Burrell was on the passenger side in the front.

As Theresa's SUV was pulling out of the bungalow's driveway, several blocks away Fuentes was looking at his watch. He was connected to Miguel by a two-way radio.

"Any time now, Miguel. I'll signal you when she's about to turn. Then you pull out into the road and block her." Miguel's vehicle was waiting in a service ally. The street Vargas' SUV would be following was one-way and narrower than a standard two-lane road. Miguel's vehicle would be able to block most of it.

7:45, 7:50, and 7:55 all passed and no Vargas.

Miguel contacted Fuentes. "Where is she? Traffic is starting to pick up. If she doesn't come soon, I can't guarantee there'll be a clear opening for me to block her. I may get stuck in the ally. Are you sure we have the right route?"

Fuentes looked a Luis. "What the hell, Luis. Did you get me some bad information? If so, you'll wish you hadn't."

Luis started to sweat, even though it was still cool. "Mr. Fuentes, I promise this is the right route for today."

Just as Luis finished, the black SUV appeared and started to make the turn. The problem was a beer delivery truck that had been travelling straight on the one-way street was now directly in front of Theresa's vehicle.

"Miguel, get ready, here she comes," barked Fuentes.

"Shit," cursed Miguel. "That fucking beer truck is right in front of Vargas' SUV. There's barely two-feet between them. There's no way I can get in front of Vargas. We should abort."

"Hell no, we're doing this now," ordered Fuentes. Ram the asshole truck if you have to and push it out of the way. Do it; do it now."

Miguel floored the accelerator of his Camry, knowing speed was the only thing that could possibly move the truck. The problem was, Miguel didn't think through the consequences of the crash. The front of the Camry collapsed and the airbags deployed, covering Miguel and his partner in nylon and trapping them in the car.

Theresa's driver was alert enough to anticipate the crash. He stopped the SUV just inches from the now tangled mass of the Camry and beer truck. Kegs of beer were now rolling around the street.

Theresa and her detail thought the crash was an accident, so they anticipated no danger. Burrell dialed EMS.

Fuentes witnessed the crash and instinctively changed the plan. Yes, two of his shooters were now unavailable, but he still had three left. Plus, Vargas' vehicle was totally stopped directly in front of him with the occupants completely unaware of what was about to happen.

Fuentes quickly issued orders. "Luis, you take the driver. Manuel, you take out the front seat and back seat guards on the right. I'll get Vargas. She's all mine."

Fortunately for Fuentes, the doors of the SUV were beginning to open as Theresa and her detail were getting out to survey the collusion. Theresa's backseat guard was the first to exit the SUV, and he was immediately shot by Manuel. However, as Burrell was disembarking from the front passenger seat, he reacted in enough time to take down Manuel with a single shot from his pistol.

On the left side of the SUV, Theresa was stepping on to the pavement when her head turned to the right upon hearing gunshots coming from that side. When she turned back she was facing the barrel of Fuentes' gun with his sneering face behind it. She had no time to react before the sound of a quick burst of firing hit her ears. She did not fall. Instead, Fuentes collapsed at her feet. Just as Theresa turned in the direction of the shot, she saw Luis raise a gun to his head and pull the trigger.

CHAPTER 38

George Washington Hospital, Washington, DC, Tuesday, January 11, Early Morning

When Mark woke up in a hospital bed, Cheryl was by his side.

"How are you feeling." she asked. "That's a nasty bump you have on your head."

Mark felt the back of his head and grimaced. "What happened? I don't remember anything."

"Apparently you didn't duck," Cheryl joked. "Some person named Horace Cooley punched you square on the jaw. When you fell you hit the edge of a desk."

"Oh, yeah, Horace. I remember now. He was mad about not being able to get to his ex-wife's – Senator Cooley – financial accounts. I was afraid he was going to attack the secretary in Bee's office."

"You're a knight in shining armor." Cheryl stroked Mark's throbbing head.

Mark was becoming much more coherent. "That's not what I remember you saying during our last phone call."

"I know, and I'm sorry. Joe Ferguson called me and explained what's happening regarding Concon. And yes, I now know what Concon is, and it's absolutely a bad idea. Anyway, Joe told me how he's being blackmailed for something that happened years ago. He also explained how other Senators have been put in compromising situations through no fault of their own. And then Lt. Evers called me, and ...."

"Evers called you," interrupted Mark.

"Yes, he was very nice and concerned about you. First, he told me about the attack and that you were in the hospital. Then he told me about the creepy British agents who called themselves Darlene and Denise and have since fled the country. He saw the photo in the *Washington Reporter* and said it was all a set-up to get you to vote for Concon. But, of course, my principled husband would not let his vote be bought, in any way. It's one of the reasons I love you." Cheryl leaned down and gave Mark a kiss on his forehead.

Mark was motivated to say, 'I told you so,' but resisted.

"Do you know how long I have to stay here?"

"You've been asleep almost twenty hours, partly due to the medication. The doctor told me once you were awake and had some food, they'd run some tests. If they all came back good, you could leave today."

Mark laid his head on the pillow and felt good about the world again, despite the trouble with Concon and Horace Cooley.

"Sweetheart, you know I'd love you to come home with me to South Carolina. But Joe explained to me about the upcoming vote on Concon. I want you to stay and vote 'no'. I want you to help save the country."

Mark received an 'all good' from the doctor and was discharged shortly after 9. He was under orders to limit his activity and rest as much as he could for the next couple of days. Fortunately, he had suffered only a very slight concussion. Cheryl drove Mark to his efficiency, made him lunch, prepared a schedule of his meds, stocked his small refrigerator, and then left for South Carolina to be with the boys. However, her strong parting kiss let Mark know their marriage was back on.

Mark went into the office shortly after Cheryl left, promising himself he'd only stay a few hours. He finally had a new secretary, Stephanie. She was a Black woman, mid-forties, quite tall, and carrying weight usual for her age. She was also a very stylish dresser, right down to her matching hat and scarf.

"Now Senator Williams, I'm going to be watching you." Stephanie had her right index finger pointed directly at Mark for emphasis. "Any sign that you're not feeling well, and I'm going to send you home, even if I have to take you myself. Understand? I promised that nice wife of yours."

"Yes ma'am," replied Mark obediently.

"You don't have to yes ma'am me, although I must say I like it. We're going to get along just fine."

Mark thought so too.

Mark flipped through his mail. More Ag reports, or more accurately, only half of each report as the Senate's paper shortage limited copying. Mark wondered if some of the Senators received the first half while others got the second half. He thought not – that would be too organized and logical. He put the 'half reports' aside for later.

The intercom buzzed.

"Yes, Stephanie."

"Senator Williams, Lt. Evers is on line two."

"Thanks, Stephanie. Lt. Evers, good to hear from you. And before I forget, thanks so much for talking to my wife."

"My pleasure, Senator. Of course, I wanted to tell her what happened with Horace Cooley. It appears I was also able to clear up some things about those female British agents posing as secretaries."

"Well, you certainly did clear up things, and it helped tremendously with my wife."

"I'm glad, and I hope you feeling better."

"I am, much better, thanks.

Evers was one for minimum chit-chat. "I'm actually calling to see if you could come down to DC Police headquarters around 1 this afternoon. I can send a car for you."

"Yes, I think I can, and a car would be wonderful. Can I ask for what?" Mark was hoping it was something about Bee Cooley's death.

"Horace Cooley is here. We've held him with no bond until we confirmed your condition. Now that you're on the mend, we'll have to release him this afternoon. I'd like to have you and him together to give your versions of what happened."

"I can't wait to be there. See you at 1."

Horace Cooley had on the same clothes as when he attacked Mark. He also had beard stubble on his face, and his eyes were bloodshot. Without saying a word, he followed Mark and Evers into an examination room. A burly guard posted himself at the door.

"Gentlemen, I want to obtain your statements about the course of events that led to the assault on Senator Williams."

Mark noticed Horace didn't dispute the use of the word 'assault.'

"Mr. Cooley, you go first."

Horace was subdued and reluctant to speak, the exact opposite of his behavior the previous day.

He cleared his throat. "Well, I came to Bee's – I mean, Senator Cooley's – office to get some financial information."

"What kind of financial information?"

"Account numbers, so I can access the accounts."

"Why do you need to access Senator Cooley's accounts?" queried Evers.

Horace hesitated before answering. "Well, I have some financial obligations, and I need to access my money."

"But Mr. Cooley, it's not yet your money, and it may never be. I'm sure your attorney or financial adviser has told you Senator Cooley's estate has to go through probate. That process will determine how her assets will be distributed. Plus, there is the additional matter of her murder. In addition to probate, nothing will happen until her murder is solved."

Horace became agitated. "But she's my wife. I have a key to her apartment. We were still having, eh, - you know – the kind of physical relationship a husband and wife have."

"You mean sex," interjected Mark.

"Yes."

"So, you attacked Senator Williams because he was preventing you from obtaining the financial account codes?" summarized Evers.

Horace calmed himself. "Yeah, well, I was mad last night. I shouldn't have attacked Senator Williams. I apologize." Suddenly Horace became assertive. "But, you know, right after Bee was – I mean – died, I saw Senator Williams snooping in Bee's office."

Evers' right eyebrow raised and he looked at Mark. "Really."

Evers continued with Horace. "Mr. Cooley, were you in Senator Cooley's apartment the night before her murder?"

"Eh, let's see, I may have. Why?"

"Were you there?"

"Yes, I think I was. So what. We had sex. It was consensual. Bee still loved me, and I'm sure she wants me to have the money."

"Mr. Cooley, you have some substantial gambling debts, isn't that correct?"

Horace became defensive and crossed his arms. "I may have, a little."

According to our investigation, you owe almost a quarter of a million dollars in gambling debts."

Horace said nothing. Things were now making sense for Mark.

"You had a gambling problem when you were married to Senator Cooley. Wasn't that one of the major reasons behind your divorce from Senator Cooley?"

Horace was still silent. He looked at the door, probably wishing it would suddenly open and allow his escape.

"Mr. Cooley, recently you asked Senator Cooley for money to pay your debts. Your creditors have gotten tired of waiting for their money, and they're now threatening you. You've been desperate to have Senator Cooley's money to pay off your losses. Isn't that correct?" asserted Evers.

"I'm not answering any more questions. I want an attorney."

"That's your right, Mr. Cooley. But let me finish so you know what you're facing."

Evers looked down at some notes.

"Here's what I think happened. You decided that if you can't have

Senator Cooley's money while she's alive, you'll get it when she's dead. You indeed did go to Senator Cooley's home for sexual relations. Afterward and while Senator Cooley was asleep, you injected the poison into her flask of vodka.

"I did not," shouted Horace, pointing a shaking finger at Evers.

"But before you injected the poison, you took a sip of the vodka. Then you added the poison and screwed the cap back on the flask. You then wiped the outside of the flask to remove your fingerprints. You started to leave, but then remembered you needed to wipe the mouth of the flask to remove your saliva left when you took the drink. You then screwed the cap back on, wiped the outside of the flask again, and left.

Mark detected a slight smirk coming across Horace's mouth.

'But you made one fatal mistake, Mr. Cooley. You forgot to wipe the *inside* of the flash's cap. When you first screwed the cap on the flask's mouth – before you remembered to wipe the mouth – the inside of the cap picked up some of your salvia initially left on the flask's mouth. And guess what. Our testing found your saliva on the inside of the cap."

Both Mark and Horace were amazed at Evers' story. Mark was amazed because it showed a clever degree of detective work. Horace was amazed at how stupid he had been.

Evers concluded. "Horace Cooley. I am charging you with the murder of Beatrice Cooley."

Horace looked at the floor and just shook his head.

CHAPTER 39

Phoenix, Arizona, Tuesday, January 11, Mid Morning

"I DIED SO THERESA COULD LIVE. SHE HAS MUCH TO GIVE. I WOULD only take." Those were the first two lines of a crumpled note in Luis' pocket said. There was a final third line. "F and Gov S together."

Maria was consoled by the fact Luis died a hero. He would be buried next to his father.

The press was mostly respectful of the Vargas family's grief. Still, there were obvious questions. Who was behind the assassination plot on Theresa? Was Fuentes acting alone? Why was Luis involved? Was he a 'plant' to keep the Governor informed? Would there be added security for the Governor?

Theresa knew it was better to address these questions quickly before unfounded rumors started. As she left the county hospital where Luis and the other bodies were taken, she approached the waiting media. Burrell, still wearing his blood-stained uniform, and four heavily armed and imposing state troopers surrounded her.

Theresa stood in front of between twenty and thirty microphones clustered together. Overhead were several audio 'booms' lowered from parked media trucks.

"I want to issue a statement addressing many of the questions you have regarding the attack on me and the death of my brother. First, I and my entire family loved Luis dearly. Unfortunately, he became involved in a radical group bent on the destruction of our great country and, by extension, our great state. At the end, he died a hero saving the life of his sister and his Governor."

Theresa waited several seconds for her information to be absorbed by the press and the listening audience.

"Second, my office, together with the state Attorney General and the State Police, will conduct a thorough investigation of the radical group who tried to kill me and who did kidnap my mother. We already have some evidence found at the scene of the assassination attempt. As the investigation proceeds, we will keep you informed.

"Last, I want to express my condolences to the family of Trooper Willis Tolliver, who died in the line of duty. He will forever be remembered as a devoted husband and father and outstanding member of our State Police. He gave his life for Arizona. Now I will take a few questions."

Theresa pointed to the reporter from channel 6. "Governor, do you have any idea why Robert Fuentes wanted to kill you?"

"To my knowledge, I've never met Mr. Fuentes. I do know he has run many ads attacking my position opposing a new constitutional convention for the country. I did not support this idea as a state Senator, nor have I supported it as Governor. Perhaps he saw me as a roadblock to his own personal views on the subject."

Next Theresa acknowledged a reporter from the *Arizona Republic*. "Governor Vargas, did you know your brother Luis was part of Fuentes' gang?"

"Only after my mother was released from her kidnappers did I learn Luis was a member of that group. But I do not know what his role was."

Without being recognized, another reporter shouted, "Was Luis working undercover at your request? Was he there to learn what your enemy Fuentes was up to?"

Theresa didn't like the tone of the questions but didn't let it show in her answer.

"Luis was not working undercover at my direction, or at the direction of anyone in my administration."

"Could he have been working for the FBI?" interjected the same reporter.

Although hinting that Luis was an FBI informant would have made him a hero and bolstered Theresa' reputation, she answered honestly. "I don't think Luis was an FBI informant, but I truly don't know. I will tell you I have not been informed by the FBI about any such arrangement with Luis."

Theresa held up her hands. "Thank you, but that's all the questions for now. You can always submit questions to my press secretary, or hold them for my next press conference. Thank you again."

Theresa and her guards started back to her waiting SUV. Many reporters continued to yell questions. One in particular caught Theresa's ear, "Governor Vargas, do you trust Governor Suarez?" Theresa wondered if the reporter knew something she didn't.

On the way to the Governor's office, Theresa received a text from her press secretary, Tim Connelly. Connelly had worked as a political reporter for the *Arizona Republic* for almost twenty years. Theresa convinced Connelly a change of pace in moving to the other side of the political ping pong game might be fun, and he agreed. Connelly's text read: 'Warren Strom will be making a major broadcast about Concon and the future of the country on Wednesday. Says he has startling new information.'

Theresa texted back, 'Put it on my calendar.'

Only a few seconds had elapsed when Theresa received a second text from Connelly: 'Your favorite friend just called and urgently wants to talk to you – Governor Al Suarez.'

Theresa let out a little laugh, the first she'd had in days. She and Connelly had an inside joke regarding Suarez. 'Favorite friend' really meant 'worst enemy.' Yet right now, there was no one she'd rather talk to.

CHAPTER 40

Phoenix, Arizona, Tuesday, January 11, Late Morning

EMILY PUT THE CALL THROUGH TO GOVERNOR SUAREZ.

"Governor, I have Governor Suarez on line 1."

"Thanks, Emily." Theresa pushed the first phone button. "Al, I understand you called me and are anxious to talk."

"I am, Theresa, and thank you for returning my call." Suarez's voice was syrupy smooth, just bordering on seductive. "Let me first express my very sincere condolences regarding the death of your brother. Coming after the kidnapping of your mother, it has to be a severe blow. Thank God, however, your mother was rescued and you were not harmed in the assassination attempt. These surreal events are being closely covered by the media in California. I think most of us consider Arizona to be like a favorite cousin."

Theresa ignored the silly attempt to create a family connection between Arizona and California. Still, she had some zingers ready to be teed up to Suarez.

"That's very nice of you, Al. Did you know my brother Luis?"

The blunt question caught Suarez off guard. "No … I don't think so … no. Why do ask?"

"Did you know Richard Fuentes?"

"I know *of* Richard Fuentes, but to my knowledge I've never met him. You know how it is, Theresa, we meet a lot of people, but never really know them." Suarez was beginning to worry. Why all the questions?

Theresa decided to go right for the jugular. "A little bird told me you knew Fuentes. And if you don't know, Fuentes was the head of the gang trying to kill me. In fact, he had a gun pointed directly at my head. If it wasn't for my brother Luis, I'd be dead now."

"That's horrible Theresa. I really feel for you, I do. But why are you bringing up these ugly things with me, your friend and fellow Governor?"

Theresa ignored Suarez's question. She now had him right where she wanted him – surprised and off-balance.

"What was it you wanted to talk about, Al?"

Suarez was inclined to end the conversation and try another time, but he had a schedule which couldn't wait.

"Theresa, remember the last time we spoke we talked about the Western States Federation. I encouraged you to think about having Arizona join. I'm telling you, Theresa, the WSF is the future."

"I thought about it Al, and I decided Arizona wants to strengthen the United States, not weaken it like your Association would."

"I'm sorry to hear that, Theresa. The Governors of the WSF think the time of the United States is past. The future is state associations with common backgrounds, common ideas, and a common future. We would like Arizona to be part of this future."

"The answer is still 'no' Al."

"Suit yourself, Theresa. But then we're going to have to talk about the Compact."

"What Compact?"

Suarez derisively laughed. "I have to remember you're new. I'm talking about the Colorado River Compact. It's expired. This means the use of the river's water is up for grabs. During the Compact, California had rights to 60% of the lower basin water and Arizona took 40%. This obviously isn't fair since California has six times the population of Arizona. Don't you agree?"

"Al, you're neglecting the fact California has access to many, many water sources – numerous rivers, ice packs of the mountains, and even the ocean. The Colorado River is essentially our only source of water. We'll stick with the current allocation."

"You may like the 60-40 split, but we don't." Suarez's tone tuned almost belligerent. "We're a growing state with expanding needs for water. Now, if Arizona was in the WSF, this dispute could be equitably worked out."

"I'm sure it could, to your advantage," challenged Theresa. "California has made a mess of its water system. You have few incentives for conservation, you've not built new reservoirs to store water when rains are ample, and you make sure your farmers are swimming in pools of water. By the way, Al, don't you have large avocado farms you're trying to protect from competition with Mexico?"

Suarez was impressed with Theresa's knowledge. She clearly saw his private interest in this public debate. However, he too could play hardball.

"Governor Vargas, California needs more water from the Colorado River, and we need it now. With no legally binding agreement, we revert to the rule of the jungle – the triumph of the strongest."

"What are you implying, Al? That we arm-wrestle? I have to admit, you've got me beat there."

"Ha, I like someone with a sense of humor. Unfortunately, Theresa, you leave me with no choice. Tomorrow I will be ordering California National Guard troops to take over control of the pumping stations along the Colorado River separating California and Arizona."

"Too bad, Al. I've already beaten you to that. This morning Arizona National Guard soldiers have total control of the pumping stations and access to those stations along the Colorado River. They also have my explicit orders to resist any attempts to dislodge them. Furthermore, I have in my hand a written order from the United States District Court preventing any changes in the Colorado Compact water allocations until a new compact is agreed to."

Suarez was speechless.

"You see, Al, I use all means to fight for my state. Only by removing me would that fight end. Your friend failed at that."

CHAPTER 41

DC Police Headquarters, Washington, DC, Tuesday, January 11, Mid Afternoon

Mark lingered after Horace was taken to a cell.

"When did you first suspect him?" Mark asked Evers.

"Here's rule number one in solving murders. If there's a disgruntled spouse, make him or her the first suspect. The twins weren't murderers. They were just put here to collect intelligence and engage in some petty blackmail. Horace clearly had a motive. He needed Senator Cooley's money for his gambling debts. He had opportunity by possessing a key to her apartment and by providing – how should I say – a regular service to the Senator. And he had the means with knowledge of and access to her vodka flash."

"I'm impressed," replied Mark, although he took slight exception to Evers calling Darlene's photo with him 'petty blackmail.' It could have ended his marriage, but largely due to Evers, it didn't. Consequently, Mark didn't pursue the point.

"Now let me ask you a question, Senator Williams. What's this about you poking around Senator Cooley's office after she was murdered? What were you after?"

"I guess I was playing amateur detective. Remember Senator Cooley whispering to me before she died, 'check the files?' I was anxious to see if I could find anything in her files that could lead me to the murderer."

"You mean lead *us* to the murderer. You couldn't wait for me to go through her files?"

"I guess not, and I apologize."

"Well, did you find anything?"

"I did. It was a letter referencing some kind of French and Spanish plan to encourage Mexico to take back part of the western U.S. I took it back to my office. But remember, that night I was hit by someone who knocked me out cold, and when I came to the letter was gone. My guess is Horace hit me and then took the letter."

"You're probably right," accessed Evers. The letter wasn't what Horace wanted, so he probably tossed it. And now that we have Horace nailed, I guess it doesn't matter. I won't be arresting you for taking evidence from a police investigation."

Mark couldn't tell if Evers was joking or serious.

The vote on Concon was in less than a week. The pro-Concon forces were making their final push. Mark was on his way to an Ag Committee meeting when he saw Joe Ferguson.

"Hey, Mark, I heard a rumor your secretary was some kind of a British agent. Since when were the British interested in spying on us?"

"Good question, Joe." Mark and Joe took seats next to each other around the committee's table. "I can only think it has something to do with Concon. I just don't know what the linkage is."

Joe lowered his voice and held a paper in front of his mouth. "So, how are things with Cheryl after that racy picture was published in the *Reporter*? I assume she saw it?"

"Oh, yes, she saw it, and initially was outraged. I thought our marriage was over. But after she cooled down and received some calls from other people confirming it was all a set-up, she came around. She even made a statement to the press saying the picture was a fake. She's mad as hell at whomever was behind the stunt and more than ever wants me to vote against Concon as revenge."

"Wow, what a wife. I don't know if Audrey would be as

understanding. At least the pressure is off you. Now that the picture is out, you can vote against Concon with no consequences."

Mark had to admit, he was relieved, but he didn't let Joe know. "What about you? I take it they – whomever 'they is' – are holding your ancient accident over your head."

Joe tightened one of his fists. "They are. In fact, I received a reminder yesterday. I got a note in the mail saying as soon as I vote 'no' on Concon, my accident records will be released, and my re-election efforts will be dead. They cited you as an example, claiming your wife had already filed for divorce. I bet there are some people on this committee, like that big Concon cheerleader Cartwright over there, who know exactly what's going on."

Mark sensed Joe was about to get up and confront Cartwright, and Mark was ready to pull Ferguson back if he did. But Ferguson remained seated.

"Joe, I heard about something that might help both you and me."

Ferguson was still upset. "Yeah, what?"

"I heard that Walter Strom – you know – the renowned broadcaster who still does a daily satellite show, is doing a special show tomorrow."

"That guy's still alive? He must be almost 80. What's so special about his tomorrow's show?"

"The ad said Wednesday's show will be the most important he's done in decades, maybe since Watergate. It will reveal who is really pushing Concon and what they have to gain."

Joe was now focused. "You're kidding. That's just what we need. This could get me off the hook and secure my reelection."

"Also, don't forget Joe. It could win the battle for saving the Constitution."

CHAPTER 42

Lynchburg, Virginia, Wednesday, January 12, Mid Morning

Tony couldn't remember being this excited since he was a little kid on Christmas morning. In seven hours, at 3 pm sharp in order to maximize the global audience, Walter Strom would tell the world about the British plan to establish a second empire. He would tell of the devious schemes, blackmail plots, and support of thugs the British had used to create dissension among U.S. states, all geared to ultimately lead to Concon and the dismantlement of the federal government. The British would then be free to absorb everything north of the Mason-Dixon Line into a Greater Canada and, globally, into the new and improved British Empire. It would be the true revenge for the American Revolution.

Carol and Tony met Strom for breakfast at 8. Impeccably dressed in a dark blue pinstriped suit accompanying a sky-blue shirt, the most prominent part of Strom's attire was his tie. It was a tasteful representation of the U.S. flag. At the bottom two-thirds of the tie were alternating quarter-inch red and white strips slanting downward from the wearer's left to his right. The upper third was a field of white stars on a dark blue background.

Strom was sipping coffee and reading over his script.

"Good morning my young colleagues, Carol and Tony." Strom greeted them in a cheerful tone. "Today we defeat the British again."

"If I can say, you look fabulous Mr. Strom," observed Carol.

"You can say, Carol, and thank you. We don't do a video of all of my broadcasts. The expense is enormous, and my limited advertisers – I should say, *advertiser* - won't cough up the money. I normally have two technicians for an audio-only broadcast. Adding video means another three technicians. But today's program is special, so we're going all-out. I wanted to look the part."

"Well, let me agree with Carol, Mr. Strom," chimed in Tony. "You certainly do look the part."

Madilyn appeared with a large bowl of scrambled eggs, a platter of sausage, and a tray of toast. "Our team must be adequately fueled," she stated while placing the food in the middle of the table.

"Mr. Strom, Tony and I have to thank you. You referred to us as colleagues, and Madilyn just called us a team. Those words mean a lot to us. But of course, none of this could happen without you. It's you that has the trust of the country."

"However, it was you and Tony that brought me the information, or really evidence. I mean it, we are colleagues, and we are a team."

Strom said little more as he hurriedly finished his meal. Carol and Tony remained quiet, thinking this might be a pre-broadcast ritual followed by the broadcaster.

Strom arose from his chair. "Sorry to be rushing off. The tech guys will be arriving soon. There are always many pre-production items to check, especially when we're doing both audio and video. Then I read the broadcast several times to get the timing right and make any last-minute changes. Finally, I have a little bit to eat and then climb the stairs up and down ten times to expand the lungs for good breathing. I know my routine may sound silly, but it's worked for me for many years."

"Not at all, Mr. Strom. Your regimen sounds perfectly logical, especially the part about exercising the lungs," commented the fitness buff Tony. "In fact, in college I took a public speaking course that recommended almost exactly the same thing."

Strom smiled, but it was clear he was ready to begin his preparation. "Enjoy a leisurely breakfast and morning. Madilyn will certainly prepare you a lunch when you're hungry. But please come over to the studio at about half past two. I want both of you there, in the studio, when I do this momentous broadcast." With a friendly wave, Strom excited the dining room.

"Thank you, Mr. Strom. We'll be honored to be there," called out Carol.

Carol and Tony finished breakfast and lingered over coffee. They thought about all that had happened to them in just the last few weeks since leaving New York. They wondered where they would be next week. Hopefully in Raleigh. They wondered if they could ever return to New York to see their families.

"I've got an idea," perked up Carol. "Let's call our parents. We should update them anyway. We can tell them where we are, and we can tell them about Mr. Strom."

"That's a super idea. You go first."

Carol pushed her parent's number on her cell phone. It was answered in two rings.

"Hello."

"Dad, it's me, Carol. How are you?"

'I'm so glad to hear from you. It's been days. Are you and Tony still in Washington?"

"No, we're not, Dad. It's a long story that we'll save until later. We're in Lynchburg Virginia."

"Lynchburg, Virginia. What are you doing there? Are you OK?"

"We're fine. We had to leave DC a little quickly. Again, it's part of the story you'll hear soon. We're staying with Walter Strom, the broadcaster. You've heard of him, right?"

"Walter Strom. Of course. Used to be the best there was, and still is in my opinion. What are you doing with him?"

"I'll just give you the quick version. In our work at the British Embassy we came across some very disturbing information. We've taken the information to Mr. Strom, and he's going to use it for a major broadcast today, at 3 pm. Will you and Mom be able to listen?"

"It's one of those streaming broadcasts, right?"

"Yes, Dad. At 3 pm today."

"I'll get Carl's grandkid, next door, to help me set it up. Will you and Tony be on?"

"No, but it's the information we obtained that Mr. Strom is going to use."

"We'll be listening, don't you worry. And by the way, another reason we were worried about you and Tony is because a couple of people from the New York State Police came asking about you."

"They were? What did they want?"

"They weren't real specific. Asked if you had moved out of the state. I know there are these stupid new restrictions, so I said no, you moved across state to Buffalo. I didn't tell them what you and Tony really did."

"Thanks, Dad. Is that all?"

"Well, one of them – the leader of the two I think – said something strange. She said that soon, maybe in months, people who had fled New York would be forced to come back as a result of some new international rules. I thought that was silly. International rules don't apply to people moving around in our country. But I didn't say anything."

Carol and Tony spent the rest of the morning and early afternoon repacking their clothing and personal items so they could start out for Raleigh early the next day. They expected Warren Strom would receive an overwhelming amount of media attention after the broadcast, as well he should. Carol and Tony preferred not the share the spotlight, but instead to begin their new life in North Carolina as soon as they could. Plus, they wanted to be as far away from the British Embassy in DC as possible. Who knows how the British might react – especially toward them – after the Brits' takeover plans were outed.

Carol and Tony were in Strom's studio promptly at 2:30. The array of electronic equipment made the room feel cramped. However, the tightness was somewhat lessened by a magnificent exterior window, probably twenty feet tall, on the home's front wall. The window let in massive amounts of light and made the studio feel a little more open and part of the outside world. Strom's microphone and seat had a clear view of the window.

Strom sat at a simple oval table with a timer – accurate to the tenth of a second – in front of him. The technicians were behind a sound proof glass wall and communicated with Strom via his headset.

Carol and Tony were shown to Strom's table.

"Greetings. You're right on time." Strom had glanced at the clock. "Almost to the tenth of a second," he said with a smile. "Please take a seat." Strom pointed to two chairs on his right.

"Please, Mr. Strom, we don't want to distract you during the broadcast. We can sit with the technicians or listen on the radio," offered Tony.

"Nonsense. I want both of you here. Both of you are part of this. And I promise. I won't be distracted. I've done, what, maybe 100,000 broadcasts in my career."

"Five minutes," Strom heard over the intercom.

"OK, time to saddle up. I've always liked that phrase. I do ask one thing – that you be as quiet as you can during the broadcast. The microphone is focused on my speech, but it can pick up extraneous noises."

Strom put on his headset and pulled the microphone to his mouth. Carol and Tony could see one of the technicians behind the glass counting down with her fingers, 5 – 4 – 3- 2 – 1, and then pointing to Strom. Strom looked down and starting reading his script.

"Good day, America. This is Walter Strom bringing you the news, and only the news, with no bias, preconceived notions, or political objectives. This is the way I've done news for over forty years, and it's the way I will always do it. Today's program is special. I will report on possibly the most important foreign threat to our country since its founding."

A noise sounding like 'whirl-whirl-whirl" permeated the room. Strom and the technicians couldn't hear it, but Carol and Tony could.

"The threat is designed to create dissension, division, and ….."

Carol and Tony heard a 'pop' and saw Walter Strom slump over. Carol rushed over to him and saw Strom bleeding from his chest. Walter Strom had been shot!

CHAPTER 43

Lynchburg, Virginia, Wednesday, January 12, Mid Afternoon

Two technicians came running and propped Strom up in the chair. Carol and Tony were watching anxiously. Strom motioned for Carol to come to his side.

Strom was speaking softly while the technicians fashioned a make-shift bandage of towels for his wound. Strom indicated with weak, curled fingers for Carol to lean in to his face.

"Continue the broadcast. You must continue the broadcast," he muttered.

The technicians carried Strom to a nearby sofa. Another technician yelled from the studio door that the EMS was on its way.

Tony moved to the window and saw a clear, round hole in the lower half. Certainly it was made by a bullet, likely from a high-powered rifle. He thought he still heard the 'whirl – whirl – whirl' noise, looked up, and saw a helicopter hovering over the house. Tony whipped out his cell phone and quickly called 911 for the police.

Carol was shell-shocked. First she witnessed Walter Strom shot in mid-sentence. Then Strom tells her she must finish the broadcast - *this* broadcast, one that could change the future of the country – to millions of listeners.

Carol knew she had to do it. She closed her eyes, took a couple of deep breaths, and braced herself.

Carol slowly sat in Strom's chair and put on the headphones that had just been yanked off the broadcaster's head. She adjusted them to fit her smaller face. She looked down at the script. It was smattered with small drops of blood. The control room operator was staring in disbelief, still reeling from what had happened mere seconds ago. Yet when he realized what was happening, he took charge and soothingly spoke into Carol's ear.

"Carol, just be calm. You have to do this for Walter. You'll be great. Just speak normally."

Carol took another deep breath and focused. She had done theater in high school and was in a drama class for two years of undergraduate school. She was always told to forget how many people are watching or listening. Just speak to one person, your most favorite person.

Carol motioned for Tony to come back to the table and sit across from her. She looked at Tony, opened her mouth, and to her surprise, she spoke. "This is Carol Shipman. Unfortunately, Walter Strom has taken ill. I will finish his broadcast."

"The threat is designed to create dissension, division, and ultimate destruction of our country. The creators of this threat are funding efforts to support a new Constitutional Convention, also known as Concon. In a free society, like ours, it is the absolute right of people and groups to support various political positions. But supporters of this new threat aren't playing fair. They are blackmailing elected officials, spreading false information, and – in some cases – they have bankrolled groups engaged in kidnapping, and even worse."

Carol paused and took a drink from the water bottle quickly provided by a technician. Through the glass, Carol could see the control room operator giving her a thumbs-up. Tony was flashing his broad smile and clasping his hands in a winner's salute.

Carol continued. "The two most important questions are, who is behind these threats, and how do I know about them." As she read the sentence, Carol thought it ironic that originally the 'I' referred to Strom, but now it actually meant her, Carol, who had originally discovered the threats.

"The answer to the first question is shocking. The British government is behind the threats. As a result of geopolitical changes in the world, but especially in Europe, the British are attempting to reconstitute a new empire. Among the planned components of this new British Empire are U.S. states in the Northeast – including New York and Pennsylvania – and states in the Midwest like Ohio, Michigan, Wisconsin and others. By sowing political distrust and conflict in our country, they hope that the new Constitutional Convention will effectively dismantle the federal government and allow the states to be – here I will use a sports metaphor – free agents. The British will give our Northeast and Midwest states an offer they can't refuse to join with Canada and other countries around the world in this new empire to be run from London."

Carol raised her head from the script and scanned the room. Everyone's attention was completely focused on her, many with looks of disbelief. Emboldened, Carol pressed on.

"And by the way. You have probably watched videos of rallies in several of our states with large Hispanic populations, such as California, Arizona, and Texas, also supporting Concon as a way to break away from the United States and join with Mexico in forming a new Mexican Empire. I have evidence these efforts have also largely been financed by the British as another way to sow division and distrust. I recently spoke with Mexican President Jorge Guerrero and he strongly denies any involvement in this underground movement. In fact, his security forces recently rescued the mother of Arizona's Governor, Theresa Vargas, who had been kidnapped by a radical group partially funded by the British."

Carol paused for another drink of water. Since she had not seen Strom's speech prior to now, Carol was simultaneously processing the information, especially regarding Mexico and Arizona, as she read it. She was as dumbfounded as most listeners.

"Throughout my long career, I have put one principle above all others – truth in the news. How do you know I am presenting you with the truth about this disturbing plot to overthrow our government? It's because, thanks to two courageous young patriots,

I have obtained the official British report outlining their diabolical efforts to create a new world hegemony. I have verified the report with my sources, and it is now available on-line at walterstrom.com. I challenge anyone to deny its authenticity."

Carol shock as she felt chills throughout her body. She really wanted to stop, but she couldn't, and wouldn't.

"In my opinion, our country faces its greatest peril since the founding. Our country needs you to fight back. Encourage you elected leaders to strongly oppose Concon, at both the national and state levels. Also demand they pass an adequate federal budget, so we can fully fund our military to protect ourselves from foreign enemies – like the British – and so we can resurrect our court system to stop invalid state actions, such as the border controls in New York.

Carol noticed Tony give her a 'thumbs-up' after her last statement.

"But more broadly, we need to take a hard look at what our political system has become. I've been around a long time, and I recognize politics is about power. But the tactics used to achieve that power have changed. Politicians and political parties constantly use a scorched-earth, take-no-prisoners policy. Compromise is now considered a sign of weakness. What in our culture made this happen? Are we now a country only of warring factions taking all we can with no compassion for those we defeat? Is this what has brought our country to the point of extinction that we face today? We need both a national conversation and a national soul-searching to provide the answers. This is your correspondent Walter Strom, at your service. Thank you for your time and attention."

Carol was spent. She slumped back in the chair and closed her eyes. Then she remembered Walter Strom. She jumped up and noticed Strom was gone from the couch. She felt Tony's arm slowly move her to the foyer, where Strom was now on a portable EMS cot and an IV was attached to his arm. One EMS worker was checking his wound while another was on a cell phone.

Jerry, one of the technicians, was already in the foyer. Upon seeing Carol, he didn't know whether to smile or frown.

"How is he," Carol asked Jerry.

"Not good, I'm afraid. With the hilly and bumping roads around here, they don't even want to risk transporting him. A doctor and nurses are on the way."

Carol bit her lower lip, but tried to remain calm and hopeful.

Jerry added, "He wants to see you."

Carol walked around the IV cord, squatted down on Strom's right side, and whispered gently, "Mr. Strom. It's Carol. I finished your broadcast. The news is now out about the British plot."

Strom immediately became agitated, lifting his right arm toward Carol and opening his mouth. She carefully moved closer to his face with her ear almost touching his mouth. Strom's words, weak but clear, could only be heard by Carol.

"You just saved the Constitution. You just saved the United States of America."

It took all of Walter Strom's remaining strength to utter those words. He slumped back to the cot, his right arm falling to his chest. Walter Strom was dead.

CHAPTER 44

Washington, Phoenix, and Lynchburg, Thursday, January 13, Morning

STROM'S AND CAROL'S BROADCAST WAS LISTENED TO OR WATCHED live by an estimated 400 million people worldwide. It was tweeted and re-tweeted another 500 million times. There were a record-setting 800 million references on Facebook to the broadcast. The full British report was downloaded from Strom's website 900 million times. Only the cooking and cartoon channels didn't reference the broadcast and report. People in the country had to be completely disconnected, disinterested, high, or drunk to have missed the story.

The response of the British Embassy was pathetic. First their spokesperson, one Samantha Surry, simply claimed the report was a fake. When that was laughed at by the media, Surry admitted the report 'could be' genuine, but argued it was for discussion only. When, at a live press conference, Surry was shown passages in the report discussing operations actually under way, she simply stammered a denial and walked away. Within hours the British ambassador was recalled to London, and the United States was threatening to end diplomatic relations with the UK.

The nation was hit with a second shock when the news came out about the killing of Walter Strom. Carol, Tony, and the Strom broadcasting team knew there would be inquiries about Strom's sudden illness. It was unanimously agreed to tell the truth – that

Walter Strom had been murdered during a live broadcast. Local, state, and federal law enforcement agencies all started immediate investigations and vowed the killers would be brought to justice. Carol and Tony had their doubts.

Carol's part in the broadcast was widely hailed as amazing, especially given the circumstances of her witnessing Strom's shooting. Several reporters had already phoned, and three TV broadcasting vans had shown up at Strom's house asking about Carol.

With all the media attention and with their commitment telling the world about the British plot, Carol and Tony decided to stay at Strom's home for the immediate future. In fact, Madilyn insisted they stay. Madilyn was devastated by Strom's murder, and she saw in Carol, especially, a link to the famed broadcaster. Madilyn had access to funds for running the Strom home and broadcasting operation. She used some of the funds to hire round-the-clock security.

Mark streamed the live video of Strom's broadcast, and like others who did, he wasn't initially sure why Strom suddenly slumped forward and then was carried off-screen. Carol's explanation sounded dubious, but Mark was quickly overtaken by the information revealed about the British plot of disruption. He was now sure the twins were part of the plot and the photo with Denise was a set-up. When he had time, he'd have to look for the hidden camera he was sure was hidden somewhere in his office.

The Strom/Carol broadcast completely destroyed support for Concon on Capitol Hill. Supporters were nowhere to be found. Several unplanned races could be seen hourly in hallways, as Senators attempted to outrun media chasing them. It was now a foregone conclusion the vote to relax the conditions for a state to support Concon would massively fail when it was taken in a couple of days. The dirty tricks played against both Mark and Joe Ferguson would now be seen by voters as badges of courage.

Busy preparing her "state of the state" address to the legislature for the next day, Theresa had not planned to listen to the Strom broadcast. Theresa thought most of his news was aimed at the elite

New York/Washington market with little content for western states. However, Emily convinced Theresa she should listen, so she took a break and had tuned in on the radio.

Although an engineering major in college, Theresa was a good student in all subjects. She particularly liked history because it took her away from heavy mathematical content and exposed her to different eras, people, and ideas. As a result, Theresa was aware of the original British Empire, and why it developed and why it ended. Theresa found the idea of a new British Empire both fascinating and scary. She had Emily download the full report.

The Strom/Carol broadcast did answer several questions about Maria's kidnapping, Fuentes, and the role of Mexico. Since the broadcast revealed the British wanted to also stir up trouble in the American west, Theresa was now convinced that Fuentes was at least partially bankrolled by them. She also wondered if there was any cartel money provided to Fuentes, or, for that matter, to Governor Suarez. She did know one thing. If there were British money linked to Fuentes, she would forever hold the British responsible for Luis' suicide.

Theresa was also relieved to hear the broadcast absolve Mexican President Guerrero of any responsibility for the movement to establish a new Mexican Empire. She could now be completely at ease and thoroughly enjoy the official visit of President Guerrero and his wife next week.

Theresa had listened and re-listened several times to the closing comments of Walter Strom – as voiced by Carol - about the condition and future of politics in the country. They gave her much to think about for her upcoming address.

CHAPTER 45

State Capitol, Phoenix, Arizona, Thursday, January 13, Early Evening

"MR. SPEAKER OF THE HOUSE, MS. PRESIDENT PRO TEMPORE OF the Senate, Senators, House members, Council of State members, distinguished guests and visitors, it is my distinct privilege and pleasure to welcome the Governor of the State of Arizona, the Honorable Theresa Vargas."

The entire room burst into ear-splitting applause as Theresa walked to the Speaker's platform, waving and smiling as she moved. The Speaker of the House, the presiding officer, gave Theresa a strong handshake and pat on the back as she approached the microphone.

The state media always covered this event. What was unusual this year was the presence of several cameras and reporters from national network and cable channels and leading national newspapers.

Allowing the crowd to continue clapping for a few minutes, Theresa finally leaned into the microphone and said, "thank you, thank you." She did this three times, as was the ritual, before the crowd quieted and sat.

"Mr. Speaker, Ms. President Pro Tempore, members of the House and Senate, my distinguished colleagues on the Council of State, ladies and gentlemen. It is my honor to stand here today for my first 'State of the State' message. It is traditional in these messages for the Governor to discuss the condition of the state and then to recommend an agenda for moving our state forward. But if you will allow me, I instead want to offer some comments about recent news and events affecting both the country and Arizona."

This was exactly why the national media was present. They would not be disappointed.

"I'm sure you are aware of several tragedies affecting me and my family. My mother was kidnapped, but fortunately was rescued by elite forces under the command of President Jorge Guerrero of Mexico. I owe him my eternal thanks. There was an assassination attempt on my life which resulted in one of our courageous state police officers being killed. My brother Luis also died saving my life. Please take a moment of silence to remember both of these individuals."

Theresa bowed her head, as did most in the audience.

Looking again at those assembled before her, Theresa resumed. "We recently learned these actions were related to a foreign plan to create strife in our country so a new Constitutional Convention would be called. Supporters of the Constitutional Convention had a goal of significantly reducing the scope and power of the federal government. While I and many other Arizonians have fought unwanted intrusions and unreasonable mandates imposed by the federal government, the goals of the anarchists – as I call them – would go far beyond these issues. They would reduce the federal government to an impotent figurehead, unable to defend the country, enforce national laws and rights, and without the unifying ability to generate the strength we have together, rather than apart. The country would fracture into individual states and state associations, ripe for the seizing by those now stronger than us."

Theresa paused and scanned the chamber. She wondered if she had gone too far. Most knew she was opposed to Concon, but perhaps she had been too bold in her opposition.

Then she heard a couple of claps, followed by more, and culminating in the entire audience rising to give her a standing ovation. Theresa noticed the media cameras swinging around to capture the moment.

Theresa now felt secure to move to the next section of her speech, the one which was the hardest for her to prepare.

"My friends, these events have motivated me to think about our country and what it means to be an American. As you know, I was born in Mexico and brought here illegally by my parents. I am a DACA baby. I have been allowed to stay in the country as a guest, but not as a citizen. Arizona law, however, has permitted me to become an Arizona citizen and to vote as well as to seek and hold public office.

Am I bitter I cannot vote in federal elections and run for federal offices? Many of you may be surprised that my answer is, no. My parents moved to America because they were attracted by its freedoms, opportunities, and rights for the individual person. Granted, they didn't emigrate the correct way – legally – and they regretted that. Yet they tried to be good residents. They paid taxes, contributed to public causes, and my late father managed a company that still has hundreds of employees. Being born here, my daughter is a U.S. citizen, and I constantly tell her this is one of the most precious honors to have in the world."

Theresa's last words were met with applause and whistles.

"I do believe the United States of America is the greatest country in the world, largely because of the genius of the U.S. Constitution and its twenty-seven amendments. And while I support immigration, it must be done in an orderly fashion using rules our elected representatives have agreed to."

More applause.

"I would like someday to become a U.S. citizen and, while I will do what I can to make that happen, I will work through the political system established by the Constitution. Why, you might ask. Because I consider the U.S. Constitution to be the most sacred political document ever developed by a people. We must cherish it. We must protect it. Thank you."

The room exploded with cheers, yells, and some chants of Vargas for President. The chants prompted one reporter to say, "It's just a matter of time. Today a political star was born."

Theresa had bared her soul, and she was relieved people liked what they saw.

EPILOGUE

Six months has passed since Strom's broadcast and death.

Carol and Tony were convinced by Madilyn and the broadcast technicians to continue Strom's programs. The response to Carol's broadcast was so strong that Strom's existing advertiser as well as several new advertisers begged her to stay. The broadcast, now done daily, was renamed 'Walter Strom's News, with Carol Shipman.' Tony put his computer and people skills to use working with affiliates, maintaining contact with sources, and keeping Carol's head from getting too big. The couple's most important news was finding they were pregnant. A baby boy, timed to arrive almost exactly nine months after their adventure in the 16-wheeler, would be named Doug after the rig's driver. Doug was now freely driving in all states after New York's and Pennsylvania's border controls were declared unconstitutional by a revived U.S. Supreme Court.

Walter Strom's assassins were never found. They were likely professionals, possibly hired by drug cartels who were afraid they were identified in the empire report.

Senator Mark Williams was a key part of the winning team soundly defeating the Concon vote in the Senate. Several political parties that had supported Concon, including the Alt-Right, Tea Party, and – ironically – the Constitutional Party, had dissolved with their members absorbed by other parties. With more cohesion and renewed patriotism sparked by the British plot, a fully-funded federal budget was passed, interest payments on the national debt were resumed, impeachment inquires against both the President and Vice-President were dropped, and a new Social Security Reform Commission was authorized. How long this new 'era of good feelings' would last was still a question. What wasn't a question was Mark's new national prominence.

Horace Cooley was convicted of the murder of Senator Beatrice Cooley and sentenced to life in prison. Senator Cooley's estate was divided among several charities and educational institutions. Plans were begun to erect a statue of her on the grounds of the old State Capitol in Raleigh.

The UK Prime Minister visited Washington in an attempt to repair relations with the United States. She claimed the British plot to establish a new British Empire was part of a rogue operation in MI6 and the Foreign Ministry. To show goodwill, British tariffs on U.S. food exports were slashed to almost zero. The Prime Minister also promised to establish a commission to explore the best ways for the UK to commemorate the 300th anniversary of the U.S. Declaration of Independence in 2076. There was no information on the whereabouts of Priscila and Daphne, aka Denise and Darlene. Natalie Tewkesbury left the British Foreign Service and signed a lucrative contract for a book describing her experiences in the Embassy. The British Embassy in Washington was downsized to its original structure.

Limited to one six-year term as Mexican President, Jorge Guerrero was being mentioned as the next Secretary-General of the United Nations.

An investigation into Robert Fuentes' finances revealed his promotion of Concon was partially supported by the British. However, the funds were cut once Fuentes was confronted by the Mexican AAE. Fuentes then turned to drug cartel money for the assassination attempt on Theresa. With Theresa out of the way, the cartel thought Concon and a new Mexican Empire would have a better chance of become a reality. There would be no southern U.S. border to surmount.

Concon didn't even come up for a vote in the Arizona legislature.

Even politicians like Tom Ellington – Theresa's nemesis in the state Senate – has changed their stripes and were all for national unity.

Al Suarez was investigated by the State of California for abuse of his office for personal gain. It was discovered he was using the WSF to divert additional water to his struggling avocado farms. He wanted to use the Colorado River in the same way. The investigation recommended his removal from office. No ties between Fuentes and Suarez were found.

Maria worked with several non-profits to establish a scholarship at Arizona State University for research on the adjustment issues of first- and second-generation Hispanic immigrants to the U.S.

Politically, Theresa was being talked about for national office. Her citizenship issue was expected to be resolved by legislation moving rapidly through Congress to grant citizenship status to DACA children. Once the DACA bill was passed, Theresa's political future was unlimited.

"Good afternoon, America. This is Walter Strom's News, with Carol Shipman. I am Carol Shipman, and today I am happy to have two guests who are credited with saving our Constitution and our country. They are Governor Theresa Vargas of Arizona, and Senator Mark Williams of South Carolina. Welcome to both of you. I don't think it's an overstatement to say each of you played a critical role in exposing and preventing the foreign plot to dismember our nation. My first question is straightforward. Which of you will take the top spot, and which will take the second spot, on the dream ticket the country is talking about for the next presidential election?"

Printed in the United States
By Bookmasters